*A
Harlequin
Romance*

WELCOME

TO THE WONDERFUL WORLD
OF *Harlequin Romances*

Interesting, informative and entertaining,
each Harlequin Romance portrays an appealing
and original love story. With a varied array
of settings, we may lure you on an African safari,
to a quaint Welsh village, or an exotic riviera
location — anywhere and everywhere that adventurous
men and women fall in love.

As publishers of Harlequin Romances, we're
extremely proud of our books. Since 1949,
Harlequin Enterprises has built its publishing
reputation on the solid base of quality and
originality. Our stories are the most popular
paperback romances sold in North America; every
month, eight new titles are released and sold at
nearly every book-selling store in Canada and the
United States.

A free catalogue listing all available Harlequin Romances
can be yours by writing to the

HARLEQUIN READER SERVICE,
(In the U.S.) M.P.O. Box 707, Niagara Falls, N.Y. 14302
(In Canada) Stratford, Ontario, Canada. N5A 6W4

or use order coupon at back of books.

We sincerely hope you enjoy reading
this Harlequin Romance.

Yours truly,

THE PUBLISHERS
Harlequin Romances

GOBLIN COURT

by

SOPHIE WESTON

Harlequin Books

TORONTO • LONDON • NEW YORK • AMSTERDAM • SYDNEY • WINNIPEG

Original hardcover edition published in 1976
by Mills & Boon Limited

ISBN 0-373-02005-8

Harlequin edition published September, 1976

CHAPTER I

Lucy ran down the lane to the village school. There was no pavement and the road was slippery with a coating of wet fallen leaves. Once or twice she skidded dangerously. She flung a harassed glance at her watch. Four o'clock already, and the children came out of their last class at a quarter to four. They would be worried as they always were when she was late. And Miss Frobisher would be impatient to lock up the school.

She had a stitch in her side and she slowed, breathing hard. Really, it was ridiculous to be afraid of the children's teacher. But she could not deny that she was. The prospect of Miss Frobisher's displeasure spurred her to further efforts and she began to trot again.

Suddenly and unexpectedly she heard the sound of a powerful car engine behind her. She had only time to recall amazedly that nothing came down the lane but the farm lorry or, occasionally, Colonel Browning's Land Rover before it swept round the curve. She leapt ungracefully for the ditch. The grass was damp and she had to cling to a vigorous growth of stinging nettles to prevent herself sliding down into what, augmented by the autumn rains, was now a swift-flowing brook.

'Damn!' she said, pardonably.

The car had swung itself to a halt and the driver got out. He looked round, saw her and strolled across. Insulted by his lack of urgency, Lucy glared at him. From her undignified position he looked immensely tall. He was wearing dark glasses, ludicrously unnecessary in the early evening murk, she thought. Behind them he appeared to be frowning. In ordinary circumstances a confrontation with an irate stranger would have sent Lucy into a panic. But now she was wet, cold and late and had had a severe fright on top of it. To crown it all the detestable man stood over her without offering to help her to her feet. He even looked as if he were laughing. It occurred to her that she must look ridiculous, like some collapsed puppet sprawled at the side of the road. She struggled up furiously.

His lips twitched. 'I take it you're all right? I don't see any blood or dismembered limbs.'

'Small thanks to you,' she snapped. She held out an imperative hand. 'Well, help me up, then.'

Ignoring the flapping hand, he bent, sliding his arms round her, and brought her very competently to her feet. He stood her up on the road, retaining a hold on her arm as if he thought she would topple over if he let her go, and began to dust her down solicitously.

Lucy gritted her teeth. 'Thank you,' she said with restraint when he had finished.

'Not at all. You were very muddy. Do you,' he inquired interestedly, 'like mud?'

'I prefer it to being flattened by fast cars,' she retorted. Glancing at the car, she saw it was of the low, sporting variety favoured by her brother. It was also, she noted with some satisfaction, liberally coated with mud.

He raised his eyebrows. 'Flattened? Do you mean you thought I'd run you over? Was *that* the reason for your dramatic nose-dive? I see. I am,' he added, by far too late, 'sorry.'

'You are too kind,' said Lucy with awful politeness.

He chuckled. "Oh dear! I truly am sorry. But there was no need for you to leap out of my way so dramatically, you know. The car stops on a sixpence and I wasn't going fast.'

Lucy sniffed. 'Speed is relative. Most of the traffic on this road is four-footed.'

He sighed. 'All right, I was going fast by local standards. I would still have missed you by a mile.'

'It didn't feel like that. I had the impression that you were definitely breathing down my neck.'

'I'm sorry,' he said again without any recognisable signs of penitence. He held her away from him and looked at her as if he had never seen such a thing before and found it interesting.

'You don't sound sorry,' said Lucy militantly, taking exception to the appraising look.

'I mean,' he explained carefully, 'that I'm sorry you're so—er—jumpy.'

'Oh!' It was a squeak of rage. She whisked out of his hands. 'How dare you?'

He was shaking with laughter. 'I hardly know,' he admitted. 'Allow me to give you a lift to wherever you're going and we'll discuss it.'

'I will not,' said Lucy smartly.

He shook his head reprovingly. 'You're not very civil.'

'No,' she agreed complacently. 'I'm late.' She looked at her watch and found that the dial was covered with green stains. Underneath it seemed to indicate ten past four. The children would be frantic. 'Excuse me, I must go. I have to pick the children up from school.'

She turned away and her forgotten stitch stabbed. Lucy winced. At once he took her elbow, frowning.

'You *are* hurt.'

'It's nothing. It's not even,' she admitted grudgingly, 'your fault. I was running and I had a stitch.'

He laughed. 'Well, that's honest. Still, I can't let you trudge on up this extremely muddy lane. Especially as I seem to have stampeded you into the ditch in the first place. Get into the car and I'll drive you to this school of yours.'

'It's not far,' she objected.

He strode over to the car and opened the passenger door. 'Get in.'

Lucy shrugged. 'Oh, very well,' she said with bad grace. 'It's straight ahead on the left. About half a mile further on.'

He settled himself in his own seat and strapped the safety belt across his body. Lucy, who had a running battle with the children to make them use the seat belts, was impressed.

'Thank you,' he said solemnly, and drove on.

The children were waiting for her. There was no sign

of Miss Frobisher. For a moment Lucy wondered indignantly if she could have locked up and gone home leaving them on their own, but dismissed it instantly. They had obviously been forbidden to go out on to the road, with the result that they were standing on the low wall round the playground. This meant that they were, at least in their own eyes, technically still within the school ground while still able to watch the road. Lucy knew enough of their psychology by now to feel sure that they would not have bothered to observe even so much of the prohibition if the threatening Miss Frobisher had not been lurking somewhere in the background.

Boy, his too-small cap set rakishly on his curly head, was perambulating the wall with his arms flung wide to balance him and an expression of intense concentration. Lucy, knowing the wall was quite three feet wide, felt no anxiety.

Angela, on the other hand, was standing still with her own and Boy's satchels at her feet, staring down the road with painful intensity. Her round little face looked pinched—with more than the bitter wind, Lucy thought compassionately. It was Angela's abiding terror that her aunt would desert her.

'Here,' she said to the man, her eyes on Angela.

'Is that one yours? The little one looking like a terrier on a leash?'

'Yes, she's one of mine,' Lucy replied absently.

Angela, at first uninterested in the car, had now noticed that it was slowing down and her eyes widened. As they drew up and Lucy hopped out she began to struggle off the wall. The satchels fell squashily into the weedy verge. Angela ignored them.

'Daddy!' she cried, pelting across to the car.

Lucy froze. Why on earth hadn't she thought what the sight of that car would suggest to the children? Hadn't she herself thought it looked like Peter's? Horrified, she watched the little tableau.

Her rescuer, in the process of getting out of the car when Angela cried out, nimbly swung round, slamming the door behind him, and caught her in her headlong rush. He swung her high in the air, laughing.

'I'm afraid not,' he said nicely, 'but lucky Daddy.' He put her down gently. 'Is it only daddies who get the twenty-one-gun salute?' He looked at Lucy. 'Don't mothers qualify?'

Angela was disappointed and, as always when she was upset, began to pout. 'That's not my mother,' she said disparagingly. 'That's only Lucy.'

'Oh,' he said rather blankly.

Lucy felt sorry for him. 'Angela is my niece,' she explained. 'She and her brother are living with me at the moment. That's her brother,' nodding to the absorbed Boy, 'doing the high wire act over there.'

'I see.' He looked from Boy to Angela. 'Well, they seem reasonably sized. We should be able to stow them and their satchels in the back and I'll take you home. I assume that is where you're bound?'

Lucy struggled with her pride. It would be heaven not to have to walk the mile and a half home with the reproachful children trailing behind. Nevertheless, pride would have won if Miss Frobisher had not chosen that moment to make her appearance.

The village school had only two classes which housed thirty or so children. The juniors were taught by a motherly lady who was as old as the school itself. The seniors, among whom were Boy and Angela, were in Miss Frobisher's class. She was an athletic young woman with exquisitely cut blonde hair and diamanté-rimmed spectacles. She terrorised her charges, even tough little Billy Marshall from the farm. Angela and Lucy were petrified of her. Boy regarded her as something of a nuisance. But even Boy did not disobey her.

'Ah, Miss Wild,' said the dragon, locking the outer door of the school with much jingling of keys. 'Were you held up?' Without raising her voice she added menacingly, 'We *don't* walk on walls, Gerard.'

Philosophically Boy abandoned his pastime and came over to Lucy, who was apologising in a flustered way.

'I was late leaving Colonel Browning and then I—er—

9

fell over in the lane. This gentleman scraped me up and brought me the rest of the way.'

Her audience reacted variously. Her rescuer did his best to look modest while Miss Frobisher turned her glasses on him interestedly. The martial light went out of her eyes. She smiled at him, looking, to Lucy's surprise, quite human, and ignored the others as she asked him whether he had lost his way in the village.

Angela slipped a cold hand into Lucy's. Boy surveyed her.

'Were you hurt?' he asked.

'I don't think so.' Rather vaguely Lucy looked down at her muddy coat. To her surprise she found that the hem looked as if it were stained with blood. Pulling it aside, she found a sizeable graze and some impressive bruising on her right knee. Boy was impressed. He was a connoisseur of bruises, but this was one of the finest specimens he had seen in a long time. His own knees were permanently chipped. Gravely he compared Lucy's hurts with his own latest crop and regretfully decided that Lucy's were superior.

'Miss Wild,' said Jane Frobisher coldly.

Lucy jumped. 'Oh! Er—yes, Miss Frobisher?'

'I'm sorry you were hurt. And of course, in the circumstances, it couldn't be helped. But you did say you were already late. That's the third time this week, Miss Wild. I really can't have the children hanging round the school till all hours. You really must try to leave on time.'

Lucy hung her head guiltily. 'Yes, Miss Frobisher.'

'After all, I can't guarantee to be free to stay with them every evening.'

'No, Miss Frobisher.'

The men took a hand. 'Quite true. And we're taking up too much of your time now we have arrived,' he said proprietorially. He ignored Lucy's indignant stare. 'If the children will fetch their bags we'll be off and not keep you any longer.'

Miss Frobisher looked chagrined. Clearly this was not quite what she had meant. Lucy, looking bewilderedly from one to the other, saw that Miss Frobisher was more than prepared to continue her conversation with the stranger, no matter how time-consuming it might prove. He, however, was blandly stuffing the children inside the car and bidding her a charming goodbye. Perforce, Lucy followed.

The children were enchanted to be driven away from school. Lucy, who husbanded petrol like a miser, seldom collected them in her own ancient runabout. Boy, squirming round so he could look out of the rear window, raised his hand in gracious farewell to the receding Miss Frobisher.

'Whew!' observed their driver, when she was out of sight. 'I'll bet she's a great disciplinarian.' He looked sideways down at Lucy. 'Did she teach you too?'

'*Jane Frobisher*?' Lucy was honestly amazed. 'Good heavens, no. She's younger than I am.'

That sideways, enigmatic look again. 'No one would guess it,' he murmured.

'Oh?' Lucy, who had been calming down, began to bristle again. She suspected an insult. 'Why?'

'Oh, this and that. Just an impression. Tell me where am I taking you?'

'Where are you going?' she countered.

'Ultimately Windrush Manor, if I can find it.'

'Oh!' She was startled. The house in question had been empty for over a year ever since the previous owner had died. The village had been filled with rumours that the heirs had tried to persuade the National Trust to buy it. It was a fine Jacobean house, small but, until recently, beautifully preserved. However, after the death of old Mrs. Appleton it had fallen into neglect through disuse. The village had shaken its head over the grounds, which had rapidly gone to seed. There was speculation on the state of the house itself. It was generally agreed that Mrs. Appleton had let it go in her last years, poor soul, and that it would cost vast sums to restore it to a habitable state. And if it were not done soon then there would be nothing for it but to pull the old house down which—again opinion was united—would be a tragedy.

'Do you know it?'

Lucy, who had spent much of her childhood playing in Mrs. Appleton's elaborate garden, smiled sadly. 'Yes, I know it. It's by the river. I suppose it's quite difficult to find. There's a gate into the knot garden that opens out of the churchyard—that's the way I always used to go in. But there's a drive which goes down to the house through the home wood. You should have carried on through the village for a couple of miles.'

He seemed taken aback. 'So far? But I thought the house was in the village.'

'So it is—the house itself. But the villagers all get to it through the churchyard or along the river path. You can't take a car either way.'

'But two *miles*. The home wood, you say. Does all that land go with the house?'

'It used to. I think Colonel Browning bought it from Mrs. Appleton years ago. But there's still a right of way through it to the house, though I don't know what state the drive will be in by now.'

'It can't be worse than your local roads,' he observed. 'I shall risk it.'

'They were cutting some trees down in the home wood last weekend,' volunteered Angela from the back. 'Rusty and I went down there for conkers and Mr. Barton told us we couldn't stay because they were going to fell that big one by the gate.'

'That wasn't to clear the drive, stupid,' said Boy from the superiority of eight years old. 'That was because the tree was ill and they didn't want it to spread. That's right, isn't it, Lucy?'

Because Lucy did a certain amount of secretarial work for Colonel Browning the children automatically assumed that she knew as much about his land as he did himself. In fact, although she had been born and brought up in the country, it was the children, new to it a year ago, who knew more about the land and its seasons, the local places and of course the local people. Lucy sometimes felt that she was living with the two most arrant gossips in a village not short of them.

'I don't know,' she said now. 'And you know I don't like you taking Rusty out on your own.'

Rusty was an amiable but overgrown Irish wolfhound who belonged to Nicholas Browning at the Royal Oak. Angela, although she loved all animals, was a little afraid of Rusty and only took him for walks as part of a well laid campaign to induce Lucy to admit a dog to Hazel Cottage.

Angela began to pout and, glancing in his driving mirror, the man intervened.

'What's wrong with the trees? Dutch elm disease?'

Lucy sighed. 'I suppose so. There was an outbreak in the copse on the hill, but I know Colonel Browning was hoping it wouldn't get down to the valley.'

'Who is this Colonel Browning? The local squire?'

She chuckled. 'You could put it like that.'

'Lucy works for him,' announced Angela importantly.

He came to the end of the road and stopped altogether. 'Now where?' he said helplessly.

'Turn right, then go straight through the village. If you would drop us at the shop, I would be very grateful. Then you go out past the bus stop and the Royal Oak.'

'Thank you. And is this driveway signposted?'

'I'm not sure.' Lucy turned in her seat. 'Do you remember, Angela?'

'Not for sure.'

'I'm afraid we're not very helpful natives,' she said ruefully. 'I never really notice the things round me. All I do remember is that it's very dark and sort of overhung with laurel or rhododendron or something. Oh, and there's a pair of old iron gates.'

'Shut?'

'Of course not,' she said, shocked. 'They haven't been shut as long as I can remember.'

'Then they will undoubtedly be covered with creeper and totally unrecognisable as ironware. It sounds dismal—like the Sleeping Beauty's Castle,' he added for Angela's benefit. Angela continued to regard him warily. 'And is the entrance on the right or the left?'

13

'Oh, the left, down towards the river. The house is pretty well on the bank, you know. That's why it's called Windrush Manor.'

'I'm glad to hear it,' he said austerely.

'Why?' demanded Angela.

'Because otherwise it sounds like something out of a Gothic fairytale.'

Angela didn't know what Gothic meant, but she knew about fairytales and approved of them. Her suspicion abated, she retired again to her cramped corner of the car.

'Oh, there's the shop,' said Lucy in relief. 'If you'd just stop here . . .'

But he was pulling across the road to stop outside it.

'There's no need . . .' she began, but he interrupted her.

'There's every need if I'm going to eat tonight, to say nothing of tomorrow morning. Or will they refuse to serve me because I ran you down?'

'Don't talk nonsense,' she snapped, embarrassed. 'It simply didn't occur to me you would want to do any shopping.'

He looked amused. 'Why on earth not? Did you think I was going to live on owl's eggs and baboon's blood just because I'm staying at Goblin Court?'

'I didn't think about it at all,' she said loftily, slightly spoiling her effect by adding, 'You didn't say you were going to *stay* there.'

'Well, I am. And, though I don't want to hurry you, it looks to me as if the shop is in immediate danger of closing. Ought we not to stake a claim before they pull down the blinds?'

'Oh, yes, of course.' Lucy discovered she was staring at him in a very rude way and tore her eyes away, blushing. She bundled out of the car and ran into the shop, knowing that Mr. and Mrs. Lamb would take due note of her arrival in an unknown car with a stranger and that neither those facts nor her flushed cheeks and bright eyes would lose anything in the telling.

She plunged immediately into buying muffins and

14

black cherry jam with a businesslike desperation.

The children and the stranger followed her into the shop. He looked round casually while she made her purchases and Boy, who seemed to feel that they were slightly responsible for the man's well-being, explained to him that he would need a substantial supply of peanuts, chocolate digestive biscuits and pineapple juice to enable him to bear the rigours of Windrush Manor. Mrs. Lamb, serving Lucy with butter and cheese in a perfunctory way, kept a smiling eye and both ears trained on the more interesting conversation.

At last, exasperated, Lucy said, 'Perhaps you would like to serve this gentleman first.'

It was accepted with alacrity. 'Well, of course, you're in no hurry, Lucy m'dear.' And she was ignored thereafter.

Although he didn't take all of Boy's freely offered advice, he did buy a gratifying amount, including a supply of potato crisps that made the children's eyes widen with awe and admiration. He also bought an enormous tin of instant coffee which Mrs. Lamb usually stocked for Mrs. Browning, who held coffee mornings.

'Do you think you'll be staying long hereabouts?' she asked, as she packed his purchases into a large cardboard box.

He looked at the large tin in his hand and smiled. 'I just drink a lot of coffee,' he said gently.

Lucy hid a smile. Although she was still seething from their original encounter she could not deny that his handling of Mrs. Lamb was masterly. He parried her every question, but so politely that she did not seem to realise that she was not actually acquiring any information. After ten minutes of interchange she had still not even elicited his name. Lucy, who had all her life been a victim of the Lambs' kindly prying, admired his technique. While Mrs. Lamb added up his bill painstakingly, she surveyed him dispassionately for the first time.

Her first impression of height was confirmed. He towered above the children in the crowded little shop,

15

oddly out of place, and she realised suddenly that he was dressed for a warmer climate. Besides his dark glasses he was dressed in denim jeans and a light cotton shirt open at the throat as if for coolness. Not much of his face was visible and the glasses masked all expression. He was leaning negligently against Mrs. Lamb's marble-topped counter, ignoring the children who were skipping round him. When presented with the bill he pulled a cheque book out of his back pocket. With it came a little book that fell with a plop on the spotless floor. Angela retrieved it.

'That's a passport,' she told him kindly. 'You mustn't lose it or you can't go home. My daddy's got one and so have Boy and I.'

'Thank you,' he said briefly, stuffing it unceremoniously back into his pocket.

Such unconcern worried Angela. 'You mustn't lose it,' she repeated urgently.

'I won't.'

Mrs. Lamb, bright-eyed, waited hopefully, but Angela subsided. The man did not seem disposed to offer any explanation of why he travelled around England with his passport in his pocket. Her eyes met Lucy's in excited speculation. Ashamed, Lucy looked away. She was as bad as the rest of the village, she thought disgustedly. As if she didn't know how painful even the most kindly-meant inquisitiveness could be.

Her gaze came back to him. He had an oddly remote face: high cheekbones, dark glasses and an intemperate mouth. It was a formidable aspect. The dark glasses, she found, were regarding her steadily. Illogically, it seemed to her that such blatant staring was rude. Deliberately she put up her brows, returning his survey. One corner of that mouth quivered and was ruthlessly controlled.

'Well, I seem to have everything for the moment,' he said cheerfully. 'Thank you for setting me on my way. Goodbye.'

The children watched him stow his box of groceries in the car with some wistfulness. His idea of essential foodstuffs seemed to them more realistic than their aunt's.

Mrs. Lamb shared their regret at his departure. 'Still,' she said philosophically, 'I suppose we'll be seeing more of him. If he's to move into the Manor, that is.'

The last was clearly a question. Lucy said sharply that she had no idea what his plans were or—forestalling further questioning—who he was.

'Come along,' she said to the children. 'Mrs. Lamb wants to shut up shop and it's time we had tea, or you'll never get round to your homework.'

They groaned, but they followed her goodhumouredly enough. Mrs. Lamb saw them out of the shop with a cheery smile. They heard the bolt pushed to behind them and the blinds were down and the lights switched off before they were out of sight.

The grey evening was darkening, not unpleasantly. Angela took Lucy's hand while Boy dashed ahead, his satchel bumping about on his back like a muleteer's pack. He seemed not to notice it. Lucy looked down at Angela.

'Are you tired?' she said.

The little girl shook her head and skipped a couple of steps as if to prove it. 'Can we go and see Uncle Nicholas?' she hazarded hopefully.

'You mean, can we go and see Rusty,' said Lucy. She sighed resignedly. 'Oh, very well, I suppose so, but not for long. Uncle Nicholas will be busy and you both have homework to do this evening.'

Angela ignored this puritanical rider and danced off to join Boy. They both then began to run towards the Royal Oak. This old inn stood at the end of the village where it looked rather like a gingerbread cottage. Its looks belied it. In fact it belonged to Nicholas Browning, the energetic nephew of Lucy's employer. He had bought it some five years previously when it was a simple village pub and in that time had succeeded in turning it into one of the best restaurants in the county. A succession of temperamental chefs and delectable waitresses had augmented the small rural community in those years so that the enterprise was generally thought to be a good thing

17

except by those diehards who did not like to see their habitual home from home invaded by, as they put it, town types. But as Nicholas was particularly careful to maintain both the fire and the service in the snug where these worthies congregated at particularly generous levels, hostilities seldom broke out.

On the whole the village contented itself with remarking, whenever the subject arose, that he must have spent a mint o' money on the old place. Which indeed, as Lucy who did a certain amount of work for him well knew, he had. Rather too much in her judgement. Nicholas Browning had a sanguine temperament and a good deal of charm which he exercised to very good effect on his creditors. However, on several occasions he had had to borrow money from his uncle in order to weather a passing crisis. Lucy could imagine that, now that the summer trade had fallen off and the Christmas trade not yet begun, another crisis was in the offing. And this time, she also knew, Colonel Browning would be very hard put to it to help. She had tried to hint something of the sort to Nicholas, for she was very fond of his uncle and rather more than fond of the amiable young man himself but without any notable success.

A faint frown creased her brows. The children were tumbling into the back yard of the Royal Oak and she followed at a more sedate pace. Of course, her position was not helped by the fact that Nicholas, who had known her since she was six years old, still saw her as a child. He would hardly listen to her advice even if he could bring himself to believe that she was old enough to offer any. As far as he was concerned she was little Lucy who had started working for his uncle as soon as she left school and would presumably continue to do so until the end of the world. Nicholas had the great gift of endowing his friends with eternal youth. Like Peter Pan and, of course, himself, they were never allowed to grow up.

There was, thought Lucy wryly as she pushed open the kitchen door and went inside, a certain irony in that. She could hear the children's voices, high and excited, somewhere in the distance. The kitchen itself was empty, although the central table was full of pans and dishes that looked as if they were ready to put into the oven. Lucy had an instant vision of the latest incumbent of the kitchen whom she had not yet met driven into headlong flight by the children and hastened after the distant voices.

They were in the snug. Nicholas, who liked to have the log fire well alight by the time his first customer arrived, had been in the middle of lighting it. The children were always enchanted by the bellows and had begged to take their turn. Nicholas agreed lightheartedly and by the time Lucy arrived the children's exertions had produced great roaring tongues of flame which filled the large fireplace and disappeared, crackling ominously, up the chimney. Nicholas watched uneasily.

'That's splendid, old chap,' he was assuring Boy. 'But that's enough, don't you think?'

'But Angela hasn't had her second turn,' pointed out Boy democratically.

Angela took the bellows enthusiastically.

'Couldn't you wait a bit?' hazarded Nicholas. 'I mean, it dies down after a bit and gets awfully dull. It's much more fun than when it's blazing like it is now.'

'We'll do it then *as well*,' Boy assured him.

Lucy came to his rescue. 'Angela, put those bellows down. Uncle Nicholas says you can do it later and so you can. But not now.'

Angela eyed her mutinously, lower lip beginning to pout. Nicholas was clearly relieved. However, he was also disastrously susceptible to brimming eyes. Quailing before Angela's reproachful demeanour, he was heard to murmur that perhaps a *little* blow wouldn't hurt.

All traces of tears disappeared. Triumphantly Angela turned back to the fire. She was intercepted.

'Angela,' said her aunt in a soft, dangerous voice.

She hesitated.

'I said, put those bellows down.'

'But Uncle Nicholas . . .'

'Doesn't want his chimney set on fire and his house

burned down just to provide you with a little amusement,' stated Lucy with conviction.

Angela turned appealingly to Nicholas.

'Well, it's going very nicely now,' he said feebly. 'You don't want to overdo it. Why don't you both go and talk to Rusty? He's in the stable because he got out and he's filthy. You can brush him down if you like.'

Mollified, they went.

'Phew!' said Nicholas, mopping his brow dramatically. 'That child should go far. She has determination.'

'She's perfectly sensible if you explain to her properly,' said Lucy haughtily. 'It's very bad policy simply to give in to her every whim, though. That way she'll never find out that there are some things she can't have and some things that are dangerous to do.'

'It might be bad policy, but it's a damned sight easier,' said Nicholas with feeling. 'I don't know how you control her. She just wouldn't take no for an answer.' He peered at Lucy. 'In fact you do look a bit under the weather. Those brats exhausted you?'

She chuckled. 'No, not really. I've been a bit behind-hand with the day ever since I got up. I was late at work and late at the bank and finally late at school. Oh, and I fell in the ditch,' she added, remembering her humiliation. 'Not a good day.'

'Poor love,' he said, taking her coat. 'Not that you're a good timekeeper at the best of times. I've spent more hours waiting at the bottom of the hill to take you into town on my crossbar than I have waiting for all the other women in my life put together.'

Lucy made a face. 'That was fifteen years ago,' she protested.

'You haven't changed,' he assured her blithely. 'Have a drink and drown your sorrows. Was there any particular reason for today's tardiness?'

Lucy accepted sherry, knowing she should be on the way home with the children but unwilling to forgo a few precious minutes with Nicholas. There had been a time when she would have plotted for days to win just as much of his attention as he was now giving her.

Today she had stopped plotting just as she had stopped hoping that he would ever notice that she no longer had thin plaits bound with elastic bands and a gap between her front teeth. She had come, wryly, to expect nothing more and to hope for nothing more. It was enough that she enjoyed his confidence and his friendship. When Nicholas fell in love—and he fell in love frequently and vividly—it was with glamorous sophisticates. And, while Lucy might have hoped to convince him that she was no longer the inky-fingered little owl he remembered, she was sufficiently self-critical to know that she was not likely to achieve the degree of elegance which Nicholas demanded in his loves. She was therefore grateful for such fleeting interviews as these and content as long as her long-standing disregarded affection for him remained a secret.

'I've had things on my mind,' she said, answering him.

'Evidently,' he murmured, sitting down opposite her, smiling.

'I've had a letter from Peter,' she said abruptly.

'Peter?' He was startled. 'You mean your brother Peter?'

She nodded.

'I thought he was still in hospital. Are they going to let him out?'

'No.' she shook her head. 'I'm rather worried about that. It sounded as if he didn't think they were ever going to let him out.'

'What?'

She looked up quickly. 'He's been in hospital a year now. Ever since the floods in which Elaine was killed.'

'In Central America,' he nodded. 'I remember. That's when you got the children.'

'Yes. Well, he had some sort of fever—it sounded like malaria or something, but they said it was rare and he had to go to the States for treatment. He's been in the same hospital in San Francisco pretty well ever since. I suppose the company must be paying for it. Certainly it's the company that sends me the cheque for the children's keep every month. That's why Peter doesn't have to write. In the whole year he's only done so about three times—Christmas, the children's birthdays . . .' She broke off, biting her lip. 'And now I've had this long screed from him, rambling on about how the children need a father's guidance and how I'm too irresponsible to be left with them except as a temporary measure. I'm afraid he may want them to go to Elaine's parents.'

Nicholas shrugged. 'And that wouldn't be such a bad thing either. They could go to a decent school instead of this run-down bear-pit here, and it would leave you free to live your own life.'

'They *are* my life,' protested Lucy.

'Then they shouldn't be.'

'Oh, don't be obtuse. You know what I mean. They're part of my life. They won't cease to be part of it if they have to go to London and live with their grandparents.'

'Forget it,' he advised. 'It takes time to get things like that organised. He didn't actually tell you to dump them, did he?'

'N-no.'

'Then save the agonies till he does.' He stood up as the door to the snug opened. He swung round and a look half foolish, half extraordinarily touching came on to his face. Lucy gripped her hands together round the stem of her glass and tried not to mind. She had seen the look before. 'Lucy,' he said reverently, 'I don't think you've met Simone. She came in a package deal with the new chef.'

Lucy acknowledged satiny hair, great brown spaniel's eyes and as sweet a smile as she had seen on any of Nicholas's former loves. Her heart sank.

Simone was polite, but clearly her mind was elsewhere. She laid a soft hand on Nicholas's arm. 'There's a man outside who wants to know how early we start dinner. Apparently he's just moved into a house and has no kitchen yet, but he doesn't want to eat too late because he's got things to do. I said we could do it as soon as he liked. Is that all right?' She added ingenuously, 'He's super.'

'Do you think so?' Lucy repressed the urge to take Nicholas into a comforting cuddle. He stood looking very much like Boy when his father did not arrive at his birthday party, aggrieved, sorrowful and quite determined to put a brave face on it. Lucy swallowed. 'I think I know the man you must mean,' she offered. 'In fact it was he who drove me into the ditch, Nicholas. He seems to have moved into the old Manor—and not to think too highly of it, from the names he was calling it. Rather a shame, I thought. It's a beautiful house. But then he didn't really look the type to appreciate it.'

Simone protested charmingly, 'He is very attractive, Nicholas. I'm sure you will like him.'

'Do you think so?' he said doubtfully. 'Well, if he's to be a customer I shall have to like him, shan't I? God knows we could do with them.'

His expression wrung Lucy's heart. Unthinking, she tumbled into the fray on his behalf.

'Attractive? Surely not?' A door opened behind her, but as the hotel was not really open she paid no attention to it. It must be the children or the new chef or even the barman arriving for once before opening time. 'I thought,' said Lucy in her clearest, most precise little voice, 'that he looked distinctly scruffy.'

'You can't judge people by their clothes,' said Nicholas who, like her, had his back to the door.

'Well, I didn't like his expression,' she said firmly. 'He was most unsympathetic when I fell down. And he looked—well, hard.'

Behind her there was a faint, devastating cough.

'I hope,' said the stranger humbly but with a wicked glint in his eye which he turned reproachfully on Lucy, 'you'll forgive this intrusion, but it was rather cold out there.' He had pulled a denim jacket over his wholly inadequate shirt, Lucy observed, and he was now huddling it round him melodramatically. 'I've been abroad a long time,' he explained, holding Lucy's eyes compellingly. 'I'd forgotten how—chilly—England can be.'

For one outraged moment she returned his mischievous look. Then, turning on her heel, she flounced out.

CHAPTER II

Lucy saw no more of the stranger at Windrush Manor in the next few weeks. Colonel Browning was trying to raise a sizeable loan to replace the Home Farm's ageing threshing machine and the work kept her fully occupied. She did not even have time to lend more than half an ear to Mrs. Lamb's inexhaustible flow of information when she bought her groceries. The village was humming over the few scraps of fact that the new resident allowed to fall from time to time. Added to that was a good deal of speculation which was by far the more interesting.

Lucy gathered that the most widely held theory was that he was a long-lost descendant of old Mrs. Appleton. 'Although Lamb thinks he's a spy—on account of them dark glasses and him carrying his passport around with him,' said Mrs. Lamb disparagingly.

Absorbedly debating the merits of haddock—nourishing—or baked beans—infinitely more popular—for the children's tea, Lucy had only been half attending, but Mr. Lamb's theory arrested her. She looked up, still clutching the box of frozen fish.

'A spy?' she echoed. 'One of ours, do you suppose? Or,' thrillingly, 'one of Theirs?'

Mrs. Lamb looked blank for a moment and then laughed heartily. 'Go on with you, Lucy Wild! You're no better than Lamb with his silly ideas. It's all them trashy films on television that does it. What would a spy be doing here, I ask you?'

Lucy considered it. 'He needn't be doing anything at the moment. He'd just be establishing his character. Then we'd get used to him and accept him as one of us. And *then*,' warming to her theme, 'some powerful politician or potty scientist or something would come and live here and then he could go to work, spying away like mad without anyone any the wiser.'

Mrs. Lamb swallowed uneasily. 'Go on! A nice gentleman like that.'

'Oh, he'd have to be a nice gentleman,' Lucy assured her, 'or he'd never ingratiate himself properly. But I bet that's what he's here for. They call them,' she added carelessly, 'sleepers.' She held Mrs. Lamb's disapproving gaze limpidly. 'Or perhaps he's from Whitehall. They must have heard that Colonel Browning has been looking at East German threshers.'

Mrs. Lamb snorted. 'You ought to be ashamed of yourself, Lucy. Making up such tales about respectable people!' She eyed her severely. 'And you've no call to stand there giggling. It's time you grew up. I don't know what those two mites are going to do for an example. For all you look so quiet and butter-wouldn't-melt-in-your-mouth, you're as great a madcap as you were at their age.'

'They don't seem to mind,' Lucy said mildly, deciding to be firm and make the children eat fish. She put it down on the counter with her other purchases.

Mrs. Lamb ignored the gesture. 'I dare say they don't,' she sniffed. 'Wild by name and wild by nature—that's always been what's wrong with your family. I've seen them come and I've seen them go, and there hasn't been one died natural in his bed that I can recall.'

Lucy interrupted the familiar litany. 'You can hardly expect me to keep the children chained to the house because my grandfather broke his neck on the hunting field.'

'*And* your father, God rest him,' Mrs. Lamb reminded her, dolorously adding up her bill.

'My father died in a road accident,' protested Lucy.

'Ah. Driving without proper care and attention was what they said, but going too fast was what they meant. It's a mercy he didn't take anyone else with him. He used to go racketing around with you and Peter sitting on his knee, till it fair made my blood run cold.'

'Well, there isn't room in my car for the children to sit on my knee,' said Lucy pacifically. She could not resent the strictures on her parent's style of driving, for they

26

were kindly meant and were, in any case, basically justified.

'Just as well,' retorted Mrs. Lamb. 'Eighteen shillings —I mean ninety pence. I can't get used to them pence, not even now. Makes things sound cheaper than they are, it seems to me. I think that's why they brought it in, so's we shouldn't notice how things went up. I mean— eighteen shillings for those few bits of things!'

She accepted payment reluctantly. It was a dull afternoon and, once Lucy left, she would be unlikely to see another customer until the mothers ventured out to collect their children from school. Lucy looked rather anxiously at her watch. She had three letters to type and post before she could, with a clear conscience, go and meet Angela and Boy. So far she had done rather well about meeting them on time, but she knew that Miss Frobisher's eye was on her and any backsliding would be met with a severe reprimand. As Mrs. Lamb slowly gave her her change she was already edging towards the door.

The curtain that hid the doorway into the little sitting room behind the shop was pushed aside and Mr. Lamb appeared at it, blinking after his afternoon nap.

'Here's Lamb,' cried his wife, triumphantly. 'Lamb, Lucy here agrees with you about Mr. Challenger.'

He paused, bewildered.

Lucy said, 'Challenger?'

'That's his name,' said Mrs. Lamb comfortably. 'Robert Challenger.'

'Leastways, that's what it's got on his cheques,' amended Mr. Lamb portentously. '*I* didn't want to take his cheques. I said to Mother, I said—didn't I, Mother? —we don't know who he is nor where he's come from. All we know is, he's living up in the old manor. But that doesn't mean anything. But Mother wouldn't have it.'

'I said to Lamb—if he's a spy, which is a silly story and I don't for a moment believe, but *if* he is, then somebody will be paying his bills, even if he don't himself.'

'Oh, quite,' said Lucy, much entertained. 'They have

27

their reputation to think of after all.' She opened the door. 'I must get back to work. There's a lot to do and I daren't leave late or I won't be on time for the children. Goodbye.'

The Lambs looked after her regretfully.

'Hasn't a moment to herself, poor soul,' observed Mrs. Lamb. 'She came running in here, just snatched up what she wanted and off again. No time for a bit of a chat. It's not like Lucy.'

'Well, I dare say she's got a lot to do, what with working for the Colonel and looking after those children.'

'It's not right,' said Mrs. Lamb stoutly. 'It isn't even as if they were her own.'

'Ah, but she couldn't be fonder of them if they were.'

'I dare say, but that's not the point. They aren't hers, and Peter's got no right to saddle her with them.'

'He couldn't help being ill,' objected her husband. 'Nor he couldn't help his wife dying like that. And Lucy likes children.'

'And the rate she's going, she won't have any of her own,' snapped his wife.

He yawned hugely. 'Oh, I don't know. There's plenty of time for her to meet some young chap and settle down.'

'When?' demanded his wife. 'Where? There's nobody here in the village, and what time does she have to go anywhere else with those children at home? She wouldn't leave them on their own.'

Mr. Lamb turned the proposition over in his mind. 'I don't see why she should have to go out and about to find herself a husband. You didn't.'

'The village was bigger then and all the young ones didn't go away to London. Who is there here now? Tell me that. Vicar?'

The Vicar was a widower of several years' standing who had hitherto resisted the attempts of his faithful parish to see him married again. Mr. Lamb chuckled.

'No, I don't say as the Vicar'd do for Lucy Wild. But there's others.'

'Who?' snapped his wife.

'Well, now. What about Nicholas at the Royal Oak?'

She snorted. 'That flibbertigibbet! She's too sensible to take him.'

'Oh.' He scratched the side of his nose thoughtfully. Then he said with caution, 'I did think as young Lucy was rather fond of him.'

'Of course she's fond of him. She's known him all her life. Doesn't mean she'll marry him. If she was going to she'd have done it by now.'

Mr. Lamb subsided. 'Oh!'

Mrs. Lamb nodded sadly. 'And she's not getting any younger.'

'Well, what about this new chap up at the Manor?' he said, inspired. 'He might do—if he isn't a foreign agent, that is.'

His wife looked at him scornfully. 'From what I know of that family,' she said, 'he'll only do if he is.'

It was not only the Lambs who were interested in the new arrival, as Lucy found on her return to the Home Farm. Mrs. Browning, in her own dignified and ladylike way, had put Mr. Challenger under review.

'Collecting a damned dossier on the fellow,' was how her husband put it.

Lucy found him sitting in the window seat of the fine old library looking worried.

'Adelaide wants you,' he greeted her. 'Some charity thing. Better leave those letters till tomorrow now.'

She protested,

'No, no, much better leave them. Then I can have a good think after dinner this evening. You go off to Adelaide—she's in her sitting-room. She got some plan for Windrush Manor, so she's been snooping.' He brooded. 'God knows what she's up to. She was burbling about a dance. A *dance!*' he repeated with loathing.

'At the Manor?' said Lucy, startled.

'Precisely. Heaven knows how she'll manage it. I mean, one can't go bang up to a perfect stranger and ask him if one can hold a dance in his house.'

'One can if it's for charity,' said Lucy in a pale voice. She had assisted Mrs. Browning before in her energetic fund-raising programmes and was not anxious to repeat the experience.

'Charity! Fiddlesticks. A lot of women without enough to do sticking their noses in where they're not wanted,' said the Colonel, a man of strong prejudices. 'Serve 'em right if the fellow kicks them out. Will he, do you suppose?' he added hopefully.

Lucy sighed sympathetically. As she well knew, Adelaide Browning's charitable activities usually resulted at some point in the Colonel climbing into his musty tails, protesting hotly but vainly, and patronising whatever function was involved. The functions themselves were of uniform inferiority and would have been dull but for the disasters which invariably struck them. Lucy, on the whole, rather enjoyed the whole thing once the committee meetings were disposed of and the practical arrangements safely delegated—again an invariable feature of Mrs. Browning's campaigns—into her own capable hands. Colonel Browning, a bluff, amiable man with a horror of appearing conspicuous, loathed them. His wife inevitably cast him as patron of her various causes which entailed him making speeches and presenting prizes. Nevertheless it was still easier to accede to his wife's requests for participation than to rebel. Lucy could well understand him hoping that Challenger might be made of sterner stuff.

'I don't know much about him,' she said thoughtfully. 'I've only met him once and he seemed—er—very self-assured. I wouldn't have thought Mrs. Browning would persuade him to have a dance unless he wanted one. On the other hand, he might think it was a good idea—to open the house and introduce himself to the local people. I don't know.'

'Adelaide does,' he said gloomily. 'She's compiled a damned dossier on the fellow. Oh, go away and learn the worst. God help us if the poor devil gives in.'

But so far was the elusive Mr. Challenger from succumbing to Mrs. Browning's undeniable powers of persuasion that he had not so far even accepted one of her pressing invitations to drinks, dinner or—a desperate throw, this last—tea. He was very sorry, it was very kind of her, but he was very busy and too unsure of his movements to say with any certainty when he would be free.

'At least, that's what he *says*,' complained Adelaide Browning, pouring out her woes to Lucy. 'I think he's avoiding me.'

'Oh, surely not,' she protested, adding, rather undiplomatically, 'He's not been here long enough . . .'

'To find out that I always want something when I ask people to dinner?' suggested Adelaide, quite unoffended. 'No, I wouldn't have thought he'd been here long enough| either. Perhaps,' she added darkly, 'Tom has been having words with him behind my back.'

Lucy chuckled. 'Or perhaps he's just naturally wary?'

Adelaide flung up her hands. 'In that case, God help us. We'll never get the Manor if he is.'

'Er—what do you want the Manor *for*?' asked Lucy, hoping she did not know the answer.

Adelaide wriggled down among the cushions in the window seat of her pretty sitting room and looked smug. 'I'm glad you asked me that,' she said. 'It's rather a pet scheme of mine. Pour yourself some coffee and come and sit down. It's in the hearth. I only made it a few minutes ago.'

Lucy did as she was bid with a surreptitious glance at her watch.

'Very well, tell me everything,' she said resignedly. 'I don't seem to have any more work to do for Colonel Browning this afternoon. But I warn you, I must leave on the dot of twenty past three or I shall be late.'

'Oh, the children,' said Adelaide vaguely. 'Don't worry about them. I'll run you down in the car. It'll be worth it,' she added reflectively, 'to hold on to you. You're my only sympathetic audience. Everyone else is bored with me. And Tom, poor darling, keeps hoping I'll lose heart and give up. But I shan't.'

Lucy could believe it. 'Give up what?' she asked, clearing a pile of papers from a brocade chair and sitting down in it gingerly. She took a sip of her coffee and looked at Adelaide expectantly.

'My Jacobean evening,' said that lady thrillingly.

'Your—?' Lucy boggled. '*Jacobean*?'

Adelaide nodded triumphantly.

'But—how?' Lucy thought for a moment and then added, 'Why?'

'Why? The Roman Way, of course,' said Adelaide, looking pained. 'Why else?'

Lucy blinked. This oblique utterance did not confuse her entirely, for she was aware of Mrs. Browning's enthusiastic championing of the old Roman road which ran along the hills. It was an ancient right of way which had long since fallen into disuse until one of the larger local properties had been left to the National Trust, which had promptly restored the footpath and opened as much of it as lay across public land to wayfarers. There remained only a brief stretch of a mile or so between the National Trust land and a much frequented bridle path where the old road lay across cultivated fields. Mrs. Browning's committee had been formed with the purpose of raising the finance to buy the three relevant fields and present them to the nation, once the County Council had established that the right of way had not been made use of for so long that it had ceased to apply.

Lucy had written all the letters and seen most of the councillors involved, so she understood Mrs. Browning's remark. But she was puzzled.

'A Jacobean evening?' she echoed. 'But what was special about the Jacobeans? Why not a Roman evening, if there has to be one?'

'Because we haven't got a Roman villa in the village and we have got a Jacobean one,' snapped Adelaide. She was disappointed in Lucy's reaction. 'Windrush Manor is perfect—especially the garden. Though I suppose we can't use the garden in winter and I did want this to come off soon.'

'Soon?' said Lucy with a sense of foreboding. Mrs. Browning was inclined to be impatient of delay in realising her plans, which accounted in no small measure for the frequency of the disasters which attended her projects. Therefore, 'How soon?' she demanded.

Adelaide was airy. 'Oh, in time for Christmas.'

Lucy swallowed.

The other regarded her severely. 'You don't want to leave these things hanging in the air,' she said largely. 'They go stale.'

'But—*Christmas*,' murmured Lucy in a hollow voice.

'Of course. We can have great log fires and the dramatic society can do something from *Twelfth Night*. The children can sing carols and you can play that thing of yours'—Lucy was the owner of a much cherished lute which, as Adelaide Browning knew very well, she constantly refused to play in public—'and we can roast an ox . . .'

Lucy rose from her seat. 'No,' she said with quiet force.

'But naturally, dear. Nicholas can deal with it,' returned Adelaide, as one making concessions.

Lucy stood firm. 'No ox,' she said.

Adelaide was injured. 'But why ever not? If Nicholas doesn't mind cooking it.'

'Nicholas,' said Lucy grimly, for she knew her beloved as well as she knew his aunt and her fondness for both of them could not disguise what painful experience had taught her, 'won't be buying the beast, and transporting it and seeing that it's cleaned and that there's a spit long enough and a fire big enough—' She tailed off, quite overcome by horrid visions.

'But it would be so splendid,' wheedled Adelaide. 'We could have a bonfire down by the river and—'

'No bonfire. No ox.' Lucy looked her straight in the eye. 'Not if you want me to organise it.'

'Well, of course, I don't want you to *organise*,' protested the ruffled lady. 'I know that would be too great a responsibility for you, dear. And when would you have the time, working for Tom as you do and looking after the children every evening? No, I can see that I shall have to *organise* it all myself, as I always do. Nobody ever has time to help other people nowadays. I never thought you'd be able to take on a great deal, but I *did* think you might take a *little* off my hands. Fetching and carrying, running a few errands—nothing that would put you out, of course. None of the tiresome committee work. But I had hoped I might be able to delegate a little of the *practical* side to you.' She sighed. Her tone said that the practical side was as nothing compared with her own bravely-borne burden.

Shaken but resolved, Lucy stood her ground. 'No ox,' she said.

Unexpectedly, Mrs. Browning gave way. 'Oh, very well,' she said pettishly. 'Though I think you're very unromantic.'

Lucy acknowledged the justice of the accusation ruefully. 'I always have been, I think,' she reflected.

'So different from Nicholas,' mourned his aunt. 'Now he said at once what a lovely scheme it was. *He* didn't make stupid objections about spits and things.'

'He wouldn't,' said Lucy with irony.

It went unobserved. 'No,' agreed his aunt. 'He has more imagination than most people.'

Lucy assented to the hypothesis unemotionally.

'Anyway, the whole question is academic at the moment,' she pointed out after a pause. 'As far as I can see you haven't yet been able to track down Mr. Challenger and ask his permission. Until you do, there's not much point in doing anything else.'

'Aha! You think he'll say no,' said Adelaide acutely.

Lucy grinned. 'Not precisely,' she deprecated.

'You think he'll put me off?'

Lucy, who suspected that Mr. Challenger's evasive tactics were not wholly fortuitous, was fairly sure that Mrs. Browning would not be offered an opportunity to expound her magnificent scheme for his house to him. She wondered idly who his benefactor might be. Clearly he had a friend and had had warning about Mrs. Browning's persistence in pursuit of her charitable ends.

'Not quite that, perhaps,' she murmured. 'But after all, he doesn't seem to work here, does he? He may just have bought the house for holidays or weekends or something. I don't think you should count on seeing him and getting him to agree.'

'If I can get hold of him, he'll agree,' said Adelaide confidently. She looked at her watch. 'In fact I'll go and see him this evening after I've taken you home. It's time we were going. Come on.'

All the way to the school she continued to talk about her idea. On the way back to Hazel Cottage she expounded to the children her plans for them to participate which fascinated them. By the time Mrs. Browning's Mini disappeared in the direction of Windrush Manor Angela was planning to let her hair grow, for, as she solemnly told Lucy, if they performed a nativity play as Mrs. Browning wanted them to, she would insist on being the Angel of the Lord. And whoever heard of an angel with short hair?

Lucy, foreseeing stormier waters ahead than she had at first envisaged, sighed and agreed.

Boy's plans for his debut were less impressive than Angela's but nonetheless fraught with danger. Boy could see himself as a shepherd.

'Oh yes?' said Lucy a little absently, as she brushed Angela's hair. 'That will be nice.'

'And I can borrow Billy Marshall's Daft Willy,' he said cheerfully.

The Marshalls were farmers who had allowed, during the lambing season, their youngest son to adopt the smallest bottle-fed lamb. By autumn it was a full grown foolish animal, firmly convinced that its rightful place was indoors with people. It accompanied Billy on his frequent visits to Hazel Cottage and Lucy had come to regard it philosophically. But she had not imagined that the creature would be introduced into Windrush Manor under Boy's patronage when she did so.

She tried to hide her dismay. 'You mean a shepherd with sheep?' she queried faintly.

Boy nodded.

'That's very—original.' She paused, gave Angela's hair a final brush and turned the little girl round. 'But

35

surely the shepherds left their flocks behind them?'

'I wouldn't have done,' said Boy stoutly.

'That is unanswerable,' acknowledged his aunt. 'I suppose we shall just have to see what happens.' She looked from one to the other of them and then said in a neutral voice, 'Of course Mrs. Browning's plans aren't always quite—quite *reliable*. Very often she intends to do something—really, really means to—and circumstances prevent her. You must try to remember that, and not be too disappointed if it doesn't come off.'

They looked at her in silent reproach.

'I mean, there's always the nativity play in church.'

'That's for babies,' said Angela dismissingly.

'And Vicar won't let us have real animals. It's just silly dressing up,' objected Boy.

'I see your point,' admitted Lucy. 'But—' She stopped abruptly. She had been unbuttoning Angela's dressing gown before installing her in bed and found her nightdress was not properly fastened at the neck, showing the edge of a vicious bruise. Pushing the material gently aside, she saw the extent of the ugly mark. She looked at Angela severely. 'What's that?'

Angela hung her head. Boy shuffled uncomfortably. 'Well?'

Silence.

'Angela, did you hear me? How did you get this bruise? Did,' with horrid vision of playground bullies, 'someone push you over?'

Angela still said nothing, but Boy seemed pleased to be asked a question he could answer with unhelpful truth.

'Not *someone*,' he demurred.

Angela glared at him.

Lucy frowned. '*Not* someone? Then what? Surely not a car? Nobody would knock a child over and not tell. One of Colonel Browning's cows,' she hazarded, inspired.

Angela shook her head dumbly.

'Well then?' They stared at her with their own peculiar deprecating mulishness which she found both touching and impossible to deal with. She sat back on

36

her heels regarding them both a little helplessly. Boy began to scratch one foot down the back of the other leg. He avoided her eye. Not for the first time she wondered if their real mother would have had the same difficulties with them as she occasionally found, and her brow creased worriedly.

'Be sensible,' she pleaded. 'Whatever it is, I won't be angry if you tell me the truth.'

'Well,' said Boy reluctantly, 'it was a picture.'

She sat down on the carpet in her surprise. 'A *picture*? At school? What sort of picture?'

Boy looked at Angela, who was twisting her hands together and showed every sign of dissolving into tears any moment. 'Not at school. It was—' he swallowed and went on bravely, 'it was up at the old house.'

Lucy looked from one child to the other, bewildered. 'What old house?' she demanded.

Angela spoke for the first time. 'The man's.' Lucy drew a long unsteady breath and she added swiftly, 'You said you wouldn't be angry.'

The breath was expelled on a long sigh. 'So I did,' said Lucy with admirable self-control. 'I gather you've been visiting Windrush Manor. You'd better tell me all about it.'

Nothing loath, now that the first confession was out of the way they sat down beside her on the bedroom rug and launched into their narrative. It was very simple and, to Lucy, quite appalling.

They had been intrigued by the stranger as soon as they met him and their curiosity had not abated with the weeks. At school their stock had soared when Angela had casually let it fall that they had actually ridden in his car. This had prompted her to suggest to Boy that, in order to maintain their new prestige, it might be a good plan to pursue the acquaintance.

Accordingly they had, on their weekend outings with Rusty, ventured up to the Manor. There was nothing in itself unusual in this. In common with all the other village children they were in the habit of regarding both the Home Wood and the Manor orchard as licensed

37

playgrounds. But they would not normally have gone as far as the house. Nor would they have tried to go inside. Mr. Challenger, encountering two muddy children with an enormous and equally dirty dog on his doorstep, had not been best pleased. He had told them to go and play elsewhere with just that degree of impatient superiority guaranteed to provoke an independent spirit like Boy's.

The ensuing weeks had been enlivened by a succession of secret sorties into forbidden territory. They had found a way into the house through a french window with a faulty catch. Just at first Angela had held back, but as they were never caught and never disturbed they had both grown braver and ventured beyond the old drawing-room upstairs into the attic rooms where the Jacobean servants had slept and which were now stuffed full of intriguing rubbish.

For the first time Angela became enthusiastic in her tale. Clearly she had enjoyed the attics.

'And was that where the picture fell on you?' said Lucy patiently.

Apparently not. The picture had fallen on Angela that very day. The whole school had gone on a nature walk and Boy and Angela, interpreting their brief rather liberally, had made for the Manor. A good deal had seemed to be going on at the front door. There were large vans drawn up in the drive and a good deal of coming and going between them and the house. The children had still reckoned their secret entrance to be safe enough, however, particularly as there was no sign of the man, as Angela explained innocently, and had entered by the drawing room window as usual—only to find that a number of pieces of furniture had been stored in the hitherto half-empty room. In particular some large paintings of the sea had been propped up against the window which their surreptitious entrance disturbed. They managed to get in all right, but in doing so they dislodged the paintings which had fallen with a resounding crash. They had fled, but not before one of them had caught Angela a painful blow on the shoulder.

Lucy patted the affected area absentmindedly. 'Did anyone see you?' she said with that grasp of essentials which the children particularly admired in her.

Angela, who had brightened during the telling, looked ready to cry again, which her brother was quick to explain.

'She squawked,' he said disgustedly. 'Otherwise they wouldn't have known we were there. But when the picture fell on her she gave a great squawk and they came in and caught us.'

'Oh dear!' Lucy thought. 'I suppose they didn't ask your names?'

Angela crept closer in the circle of her arm.

'Well, not exactly,' allowed Boy. 'But they asked us what we were doing and we said we were on a nature walk. And they said,' he finished miserably, 'that they would see Miss Frobisher.'

'Oh *dear*!' said Lucy with feeling. 'And we aren't too popular with Miss Frobisher anyway. Oh well, I suppose it can't be helped. Did you notice if there was any damage to the picture at all?'

'We couldn't lift it,' volunteered Angela, rubbing a forefinger round her eyes. 'We were going to stand it up again,' she explained, 'and pretend we'd never been there. Only it was too heavy.'

Lucy frowned worriedly. 'In that case it might have hurt you badly.' She inspected the bruise closely but could see no signs of undue discolouration or that her gentle proddings caused Angela to wince more than she would have expected. 'Can you move your arm?'

Angela swung her arms energetically, windmill-fashion.

'Yes, I can see you can,' said Lucy, not quite dodging in time. Her hair was sent flying wildly by a glancing blow. She shook it out of her eyes. 'Does your shoulder hurt? Is it stiff?'

Again Angela experimented.

'Only when I press it,' she decided at last, suiting her action to words and wincing dramatically.

'Then you'd best go to bed now,' said Lucy, 'and we'll

see how it is in the morning. If it hurts, we'll go to Dr. Fraser. But for now—bed.'

Nothing loath, Angela scrambled off the hearthrug and into bed among an impressive row of stuffed animals. Her favourite was a rather battered panda with uneven eyes, as he had lost one on a trip to London and had to have it replaced by one of a different shade which was all Lucy's button box had to offer. Angela, a philosophical child, said it made him special and loved him all the more. Nevertheless, Lucy knew that she felt he was not quite as beautiful as before and therefore always now allotted him pride of place in her nursery menagerie so that he should not feel hurt. Lucy annually knitted him waistcoats and made him nightshirts that matched Angela's own nightdresses for the same reason.

Panda was now therefore solemnly taken out of his cherry red waistcoat and put into night attire and then tucked in beside Angela. Boy and Lucy kissed them both goodnight and Boy went to his own room. Lucy lit the nightlight, put it on top of the wardrobe so it should not shine in Angela's eyes, and left quietly. In five minutes, she knew, Angela would be fast asleep.

Not so Boy. He went to bed every evening surrounded by paper and crayons and all manner of necessary flotsam with which he announced himself to be drawing. He then fell asleep in stages. Lucy usually found herself picking acorns or bits of bark off his eiderdown and drawing the bedcovers up about his ears when she went to bed herself. And changing his sheets regularly produced a shower of pencils that had been lost during his artistic activities.

Tonight, however, he did not want to draw but went straight to bed with uncharacteristic quietness.

'Do you want some hot chocolate?' asked Lucy, concerned.

He turned over with his back to her and locked his arms round his knees. He shook his head.

'Are you sure?' she persisted.

Again a silent headshake.

'Very well.' She went to the door, after brushing his

40

averted cheek with her lips. 'Do you want me to leave the door open?'

Boy had long since given up nightlights, but he did have occasional bouts of disliking the dark.

'No, thank you,' he said politely.

'All right,' said Lucy, feeling helpless again and rather worried. 'But call out if you want anything.'

She went downstairs thoughtfully. Boy had obviously got a guilty conscience because he had led Angela into an escapade which looked as if it might have dire repercussions for them all. Angela was still at the age when she could find release in confession and a hearty bout of tears, but Boy was sufficiently grown up to realise that 'I'm sorry' was not the magical panacea that his sister supposed it to be. Lucy remembered making that painful discovery for herself and sympathised. She hoped he was not really fearful of retribution. Of course, they had been naughty, but as far as she could see they had done no real damage. She could not really imagine the man she had met filled with righteous wrath at the children's adventures. If it had been the Colonel now, who thought that children, like puppies, should stay out of doors where they could do no harm, the case would be very different. Or even the Vicar, though he conscientiously tried to enter into the pastimes of his younger congregation, might have taken the occasion to deliver a few grave words on the subject of respecting other people's property. But Challenger—! Lucy tried to imagine that young man delivering a lecture to the children and giggled. He had far more the appearance of one who would show them how not to get caught next time.

She switched on the table lamp and settled down with the accumulated tears, scuffs and wrenched seams of the children's weekly washing. She was still busy congratulating herself that she need not expect a visit from an irate householder, with one ear open for sounds of distress from the children's rooms, when she was startled by a resounding knock at the door.

Puzzled, she pushed aside her workbasket and went

41

to open it.

On her doorstep, wet and windswept and clearly furious, stood Robert Challenger.

'Oh,' said Lucy in a pale voice, her hand falling from the door. She cast a nervous look up the stairs, but as far as she could see Boy's door remained firmly shut. She squared her shoulders. Obviously the man was going to be unpleasant and she must do her best to shield the children from what was, equally obviously, a far from sweet temper. She swallowed. 'You'd better come in.'

Almost furtively she shepherded him round the staircase and out of earshot of the children, firmly closing the sitting-room door behind him.

'I—' he began, but she hushed him unceremoniously until she had closed the door.

He watched her, an arrested expression on his face. Anger gave way to that deplorably superior amusement she had seen before.

'Enemy active tonight?' he hissed in a stage whisper, his mouth solemn.

Lucy looked at him with dislike. 'I just don't want to disturb the children,' she said softly.

He was taken aback. 'Er—no, I suppose not,' he whispered back. 'Do you think it would disturb them if we talked normally? This muttering is very painful on the larynx.'

'Of course,' said Lucy with disdain, in her ordinary voice. 'It doesn't matter now the door's shut. I just didn't want to let Boy hear you if he should happen to be awake.'

His eyebrows flew up. 'Boy?'

'My nephew,' explained Lucy. She sat down on the arm of a shabby chair and sighed. 'You have met,' she added sadly.

'Oh yes, so we have.' He did not seem disposed to continue the subject but stood looking down at her, half-smiling. 'Doesn't he like you having callers after dark?'

She snorted. 'Don't be flippant. The poor child's been in an absolute fever waiting for you to turn up all day.'

It was an exaggeration, but it was a subject on which she felt strongly.

'Has he?' he said, fascinated. 'How very perspicacious of him. Tell me, does he have second sight? Or is he the little monster who scatters broken milk bottles in the road to rip up the tyres of the unwary traveller?'

'He's *not* a little monster,' she fired up. 'He's just an ordinary mischievous child and—*what* did you say?'

His mouth twitched. 'Milk bottles,' he said gently. 'Broken milk bottles. They're strewn all over the road out there, with the result that my car has not one but three flat tyres. I wanted to use your telephone if I might.'

'Oh,' she said weakly. She could see, now that she looked, that his fingers were covered in black grease. He must have changed, or begun to change, one tyre before he discovered the state of the others. That would account for the expression of black fury on his face. A treacherous desire to laugh rose in her, but she sternly suppressed it. 'Of—of course,' she said, only the slightest tremor in her voice. She indicated the telephone on a bookcase in the corner of the room. 'Over there. If you want the garage in the village the number's on the pad.'

He looked at her narrowly.

'I'll—I'll make you some coffee while you're phoning,' she gasped. 'I'm sure you're wet and cold.'

And escaping to the kitchen she gave way to a paroxysm of mirth.

She was wiping her eyes on a convenient drying-up cloth when she became aware of being watched. Robert Challenger was standing ominously in the doorway. From his attitude, one arm negligently on the frame above his head, one foot crossed in front of the other, she inferred he had been there for several seconds, and therefore had witnessed her unseemly fit of the giggles. Still choking intermittently on a nervous laugh, she gave a final defiant wipe to her eyes and faced him.

'Do you always laugh so immoderately at other people's disasters?' he demanded, surveying her.

43

She hiccuped. 'N-not invariably.'

'I think you must be mad,' he said, as one making a discovery. 'First of all you spirit me into the house as if it were being watched by the Special Branch. Then you claim your nephew has foretold my coming and now I find your having hysterics in the kitchen.'

She chuckled. 'I'm sorry. It must look strange, I know . . .'

'It does,' he assured her. 'At least to me. But then I'm a comparative newcomer. A good deal of what goes on in this village seems strange to me. I'm not sure I shall survive the pace of rural life. The people in the little shop clearly suspect me of dark doings up at Dracula's Palace . . .'

Lucy giggled again at his unflattering reference to his house.

He went on, ignoring her, 'Both the Colonel's lady and the Vicar track me down remorselessly—why, I can't imagine. There's you, who are clearly unhinged. And today my house was invaded by some lethal tots who did their best to demolish the only decent painting in the place.'

'How—how unfortunate,' said Lucy airily.

He looked at her suspiciously.

'Was it very valuable?' she added hastily, not quite keeping the anxiety out of her voice.

His eyes widened in comprehension. 'I *see*,' he said softly. '*Your* lethal tots.'

For a craven moment Lucy was tempted to deny it. After all, if he wasn't sure and had no proof, he could hardly persecute the children. Only the thought of explaining her dissimulation to Boy prevented her. Her nephew's uncomfortable conscience extended to his immediate family, and he was at the age to be very severe with Lucy's evasions. She stopped laughing and hung her head.

'I'm afraid so,' she agreed. 'Was the painting very valuable? I do hope they didn't do any irreparable damage. From what Boy told me, I thought they'd come off rather the worse in the encounter.'

44

He frowned quickly. 'You mean the child was hurt?'

'Angela was a little. That's how I found out. She couldn't explain the bruise away, so I made her tell me the truth. It doesn't look as if it's much.'

'Has she seen a doctor?'

'I hardly think . . .'

'I can well believe it,' he said unkindly. 'For heaven's sake, woman, that painting had been in the attic for a hundred years or more. God knows what bugs it carried.'

Lucy eyed him with hostility. 'I am well aware of the dangers,' she said frostily. 'However, I don't lose my head every time one of the children bumps his knee. Angela had a bruise, but the picture hadn't broken the skin. Therefore she has a sore shoulder and a good fright, neither of which is likely to prove fatal. What I'm more interested in is the damage to your picture. You must of course allow me to pay for it.'

He dismissed it. 'That's nonsense.'

'I,' said Lucy militantly, 'insist.'

He began to look harassed. 'Well, I don't know how much it will cost, or even if I can find anyone to repair it.'

Lucy subsided, torn between guilt and an obscure feeling of dissatisfaction with the man. It was as if he did not take her seriously. He might be joking when he said she was mad, but he had not been laughing when he berated her for not taking Angela instantly to the doctor. What business was it of his? she thought resentfully. Yet one did not like to appear foolishly irresponsible in anybody's eyes, even those of a worldly and indifferent stranger.

'Well, if you can find someone to do it, you must send the bill to me,' she pursued, rather sulkily.

He sighed. 'Oh, very well. And now please may I wash my hands?'

'What?' She stared at him nonplussed. He waved grimy hands under her nose and she took a step backwards. 'Oh! Of course.'

'Then perhaps I can telephone the garage to come and collect my car. At present it's lurching drunkenly up against your hedge.'

Lucy gave him soap and a towel without comment.

'Thank you.'

He went back into the sitting-room and she heard him talking on the telephone while she filled the ancient percolator and set it on the stove. When he returned to the kitchen there was a delicious smell of coffee.

He did not appear to appreciate it. 'The old fool says the car will have to stay there till morning.'

'I thought he would,' said Lucy serenely, putting mugs on a tray. 'Are you hungry?'

'Yes. What do you mean you thought he would? Why didn't you say so?'

'Because I wasn't sure. And anyway, he might have come out for you. He won't for me. He's a curmudgeonly soul and he doesn't approve of women drivers. So it's a sort of triumph for him when my car breaks down.'

'He doesn't approve of foreign sports cars either,' he said ruefully. 'Or the people who drive them.'

'Oh well,' said Lucy philosophically. 'It could be worse. When you've finished I'll get the car out and drive you back to the Manor. How hungry are you? Cheese sandwich hungry or do you want a proper fry-up?'

He looked at her in amazement. 'Are you proposing to feed me?'

For some unaccountable reason Lucy blushed. 'Well, you're wet and cold,' she said gruffly. 'It's a horrible night.'

'It is indeed.' He took the tray from her as she began to butter large slices of crusty bread. 'And not made any better, I imagine, by me stamping in here and—er—disturbing the children. This is very charitable of you.'

'I'd do the same for anybody,' Lucy assured him untruthfully, conveniently forgetting Jane Frobisher and the Howards from the garage. 'If the truth is known it's probably my milk bottle that's the cause of the trouble. We put them in the hedge so the milkman doesn't have to come all the way up to the house to deliver, but it's not really satisfactory. I think one must

46

have rolled out tonight—there's a strong wind up. I'd better go and brush the pieces out of the road before somebody else comes to grief.'

She put the plate of sandwiches on the tray and said, 'Go and sit by the fire and have your coffee. It won't take a minute.'

He handed the tray back to her, laughing. 'I hope not. But it won't take *me* a minute. I'm dressed for the weather.'

He took the broom from her resistless hand and marched to the front door. Inside five minutes he was back, taking off his thick duffle coat and clapping his hands together to bring the blood back into them. Lucy drew a stout old chair to the fire for him and poured steaming coffee into a mug.

'There you are,' she said as she would have done to Boy or Angela. 'You shouldn't have gone out again. You've probably caught pneumonia or something. And it was almost certainly my fault that the horrid thing smashed anyway. What with your car and your painting I seem to put a jinx on your possessions.'

He made deprecating noises through a mouthful of cheese sandwich.

'And you've been very considerate,' she continued, determined to be diplomatic. 'About the children and everything. I'm rather deeply in your debt.'

She gave him what she hoped was an appealing look. He would disclaim and then she would ask him to forgive the children. But her policy proved vain.

He returned her look quizzically.

'Yes, you are, aren't you?' he agreed.

CHAPTER III

There was a stunned silence while Lucy tried to think of a dignified retort. At last she abandoned the attempt.

'There's no need to sound so *pleased* about it,' she said crossly. 'Anyone would think you welcomed having your goods and chattels destroyed.'

He considered it, eyes half-closed. 'No, I don't think I would say that,' he demurred. 'Not *welcomed* exactly. But I am not altogether opposed to having you in my debt.'

Lucy eyed him suspiciously. The remark sounded faintly threatening in some way which she did not choose to explore.

'Why?' she demanded.

He seemed to be debating his reply. He stretched comfortably in the old chair, sinking deeper into its battered cushions and letting his eyelids droop until Lucy began to wonder seriously whether he was falling asleep under the combined influences of the warm fire and her awkward questions.

When he eventually spoke, it was irrelevantly. 'This is a remarkably pleasant room,' he murmured.

'Thank you,' she said, sitting a little straighter in her chair and fixing him with an imperative eye. '*Why* do you want me in your debt?'

His eyelids lifted and he smiled at her lazily. 'As a sort of tactical move,' he explained with a great air of frankness.

'Tactical?' Lucy was now utterly lost. 'I wish,' she said roundly, 'you'd stop making oblique threats and tell me whatever it is.'

He sighed. 'And I was so comfortable. I warn you, you won't like it. Will you throw me out the moment I've finished and never let me darken your door again?'

He looked so comically anxious, clutching a coffee mug

48

protectively to his shirt front, that Lucy found her errant
sense of humour betrayed her again. She began to laugh.

'Very probably,' she agreed. 'Do you want indemnity
before you begin? Very well,' she said as she had said to
Boy earlier that evening, 'if you tell me the truth, I
won't be angry with you.'

'Ah, but can I rely on that?' he murmured provoca-
tively.

'I would think so,' she retorted. 'If the children fail to
induce me to lose my temper and break my promises of
forbearance then I shouldn't think you could do so.'

'A comforting thought,' he said ironically.

He put his cup down but, in spite of the fact that he
was smiling, she thought she could still detect the vestiges
of several less pleasant expressions in his face. His mouth
had taken a rather hard line and she suspected that,
behind the dark lenses, his eyes were grim. She quelled a
flutter of nervousness and folded her hands in her lap.

'First of all, I'd better introduce myself.'

She looked blankly at him. 'But I know your name,'
she pointed out.

His mouth relaxed. 'And that's enough?' he asked,
amused.

She nodded. 'Unless you want to show me your
driving licence or your police badge or something,' she
added, remembering Mr. Lamb's flights of fancy.

'My *what*?'

'Or your CIA identity card,' she expanded, and began
to laugh at his expression.

'You *are* mad,' he said with great calm. 'I knew you
were.'

'No, no. Or if I am, it's a madness many a respectable
man shares. Well,' she added fairly, 'one respectable
man.' She giggled helplessly while he watched her with
ostentatious patience. 'I'm sorry.' She wiped her eyes.
'You see, Mr. Lamb—you know, Mr. Lamb at the
village shop—will have it that you're not what you
seem. He thinks you're a secret agent but hasn't made
up his mind which side you're on.'

His face relaxed and he laughed softly. 'And you

49

plumped for the CIA. Why?'

'Ah, well,' began Lucy enjoyably, 'when you first arrived it didn't look to me as if you'd just flown in from the frozen wastes of Russia. Not the way you were dressed. Hence the CIA.' She sat back, pleased with herself.

His mouth twitched. 'Chopped logic, my child. I could have been spying for the KGB in the West Indies. You shouldn't judge by appearances.'

'I didn't think of that,' said Lucy, crestfallen.

'You will next time,' he said kindly. 'Is there any more coffee?'

She picked up the percolator and swirled it experimentally. 'I don't know how hot it is,' she warned, filling the mug he held out to her. 'Did you really come here to confess that you're an international spy?' she asked, interesed.

'Would you believe me, if I said yes?'

She pondered. 'I wouldn't have any reason to disbelieve you,' she opined. 'So yes, I dare say I would.'

He surveyed her, half-smiling. 'You tempt me, you really do. But I cannot tell a lie to such trusting innocence. I'm a mere engineer, quite ordinary and unexciting.'

Lucy thought of the reaction to his arrival in the village and suppressed a chuckle, contenting herself with a modest, 'I wouldn't say that.'

'Oh, I assure you. I spend most of my days closeted with a drawing board and a slide rule.'

'And the West Indies?' murmured Lucy.

'I'd been building a bridge there,' he acknowledged. 'What a little sleuth you are!'

'Bridges?' Her head jerked up. 'But that's what my brother does. He works for a big contractor, though, he's not freelance.'

'We call them consultants,' he said primly. 'Yes, I know about Peter. I've—'

'Met him?'

'Worked with him,' he corrected. 'In fact I worked with him in Honduras. I even stayed with him and

50

Elaine before the floods in which she died.'

'*Did* you?' Lucy was more bewildered than ever. 'But why didn't you say so at once? And what coincidence brought you here . . .?' Her voice trailed off. 'It wasn't coincidence, was it?' she said quietly.

'I'm afraid not.'

She stood up and went to the window staring out unseeingly into the dark garden with the darker lane beyond. Dimly she could see a faint glow which she supposed must be the lights of his car. She wrapped her arms across her body, surprised to feel the coldness of her own hands. Her throat was dry. He had come to tell her she must send the children to their grandparents. That they were old and fussy and driven to exasperation by more than three or four hours of the children's company didn't matter. Peter had decreed their future and Peter was their father. And, with that deadly efficiency that he had brought to organising all their childish games as she remembered, he had not committed his orders to paper but had sent a messenger charged with instructions to turn all their lives upside down.

'Go on,' she said in a chill little voice.

'I'd rather you came back and sat down. It's not easy.'

'Is that why you've put it off for— how long? Three weeks, is it? Couldn't you face me before?' she flashed.

He looked rueful. 'Well, I hardly got an enthusiastic reception. And that was even before you knew who I was.' He stood up. 'Look, we can work something out. Don't get upset.'

He came towards her. Lucy whipped round, bracing herself.

'I am not,' she said determinedly, 'upset. I gather Peter has asked you to deliver the children to their grandparents. I have nothing to say except that I shan't do anything until I've written to Peter. Do I make myself clear? And now perhaps you'll go.'

He ignored her, taking her hands and urging her on to the window seat. 'Stop shaking,' he said kindly. 'Peter didn't tell me to do anything of the kind, and if he had I wouldn't have agreed. Stop torturing yourself.

What on earth gave you such an idea?'

'You—you wouldn't?' She drew the back of a shaking hand across her mouth in a childish gesture which returned in moments of stress. 'But—Peter said—I mean, I had a letter from him . . .'

'Then he must have explained.'

She shook her head. 'No. It—well, it was rather vague, I suppose. I took it to mean he wanted the children to go back to Elaine's parents. He was complaining about the village school. Oh yes, and he said Boy needed a stable father figure in his life.' She sniffed sorrowfully. 'What else was I to think?' she demanded, aggrieved.

'Did he indeed?' He sounded startled. Then he released her hands. 'I see your confusion. Peter doesn't seem to be any better at explaining himself than I am. He gave me a letter to deliver to you which I hope says it all better. But it would probably be best to give you a brief run-down first—then at least I can stop you jumping to unwelcome conclusions,' he added dryly.

He went back to the fire and stood, with his hands behind his back, looking into the flames. 'I don't know quite how to put it. It sounds rather insulting. You see, Peter's worried about the children. They've done lots of tests on him—and they're doing more. He's not in bed all the time or anything drastic like that. It's simply that he can't shake off this infection and the doctors haven't identified it yet. Apparently he's been fretting badly at the lack of progress. That's why I was —er—asked to go and see him.'

She stared at him.

'He was—very excited. He said that something permanent had to be done about the children, that they couldn't go on living as temporary guests with you. He didn't think it was fair to you, among other things. So he suggested—that—' He took a deep breath and said simply, 'He wants them to go away to school.'

'Away?' Lucy was uncomprehending. 'You mean boarding school? *Both* of them? But they're so little. They'd hate it. Oh, he can't do that!' She rose angrily to her feet. 'And you can't do that. I won't let you. I'll telegraph Peter. I'll see my lawyer tomorrow. You *can't* . . .'

'I can,' he said calmly. 'Or rather, I could if I judged it right. Peter has made me their guardian in his absence from England. I showed the deed to my solicitor as soon as I got back to England—that's really why I haven't spoken to you before. I wanted to know what our respective legal positions were. My solicitor says that he thinks you have a good case if you want to fight it. Courts are usually sympathetic to women parted from their ewe-lambs, apparently.'

Lucy flung her head up at that. 'Don't you dare to sneer at me!' she whispered.

'I'm not sneering. God knows, I don't blame you for feeling bitter.' He sounded very tired. 'I'm just trying to point out that you aren't helpless. You do have some redress if you feel that strongly. But—I'm told—the process is slow and costly. It would be better for everyone, not least the children, if we can come to some sort of arrangement.'

Lucy found humiliatingly that she wanted to cry. She turned her back on him, groping for a handkerchief. 'What sort?'

Robert Challenger laughed, heartlessly she thought. 'I hardly think there'd be any point in discussing it tonight. You're not in a mood to agree to anything. You'll be sticking pins in a wax image of me as soon as I've gone out of that door. Leave it till tomorrow. I'll come and see you.'

'I don't want to see you again,' she snapped childishly.

'I'm sure you don't,' he said with maddening sympathy. 'But that's hardly practical, is it? I'll leave you Peter's letter.'

He held it out to her, but she kept her back firmly turned away. Sighing, he put it on the arm of a chair.

'Coincidence!' she said bitterly. 'I don't believe in it. What about those milk bottles? I bet you broke them yourself just to have an excuse to get in here. And the house—how did you come to buy a house here?'

53

He shrugged. 'Dracula's Palace?'

'Don't call it that,' she snapped. 'It's beautiful.'

'It's old,' he allowed. 'Oh, come on, be sensible. We can't fight about a house.'

'It's a lovely old house. I suppose you can't appreciate it.'

'It has been,' he said pacifically. 'Now it's damp, it's got dry rot which the whole place reeks of, it's filthy and it's infested with rats.'

'So why buy it?'

He grinned. 'It appeals to my romantic soul.'

'You bought it so you could come and spy on me, didn't you? Is Peter paying for it?'

He strode forward and swung her round by the shoulders. 'Enough,' he said grimly, 'is enough. I make every allowance for your natural shock—' He saw the tears trickling down her cheeks and added in more moderate tones, 'I wanted a house. I've no ties in England. This seemed a nice enough place and Dracula's Palace took my fancy. Anyway, it's natural enough to want to be near the children, isn't it, if I'm responsible for them?'

'You are not,' she said between her teeth, 'responsible for them.'

'In law I am. And financially I am. Trust funds are being set up for them, and I shall be a trustee.'

For a speechless moment she looked up into his calm face. Behind the glasses he seemed to be laughing at her. She took a step back out of his imprisoning hands and, very deliberately, dealt him a ringing blow. The back of her hand smarted. She cradled it in the other one, appalled, waiting for retribution that she was sure would follow.

The glasses glittered down at her. He had seen it coming and dodged, but not quickly enough, and there was now a dull red mark along his cheek. For a brief moment she held her breath.

Then he said with great control, 'You're upset. I'll leave you. But if you ever try to do that again, I shall return it with interest.'

54

She backed away. 'I'm sure you would,' she said with disdain. 'However, the occasion won't arise. I shan't touch you again. I'm sorry I—forgot myself.'

'So am I,' he said ruefully. Then he smiled at her forgivingly. 'Never mind, I'm sure I deserved it. Let's say we're quits and start again. Can't we be friends?'

She snorted. 'Hardly.'

Unexpectedly he took her face between his hands. 'You know, you're a termagant,' he informed her. 'And Peter told me you were a quiet little thing who wouldn't give me any trouble. He underestimated you.'

'I hope so,' she returned viciously. 'I have every intention of giving you as much trouble as I can.'

'I can well believe it.' His mouth suddenly twitched in that unexpected, disrespectful laughter with which she was becoming familiar. 'Oh well, in for a penny,' said Robert Challenger cheerfully, and kissed her.

Simple amazement held her still. She was still standing, dazed, when she heard the front door close gently behind him.

Lucy opened her eyes—which she could not recall having shut—swallowed and sat down shakily. The man was, of course, quite insufferable. He was impertinent, interfering and, to crown it all, he did not even seem to take her seriously. How dared he treat her as if she were some little mouse to sit quietly at home while he and Peter arranged her life to suit themselves! He had not even listened to her objections. Above all, how dared he walk out on that light, insulting kiss as if that was all that was needed to pacify her?

For a moment the greater issue was lost in the lesser one as she sat and fumed. Then common sense prevailed and she stretched out her hand for the letter. It was written on thin airmail paper and the envelope had the title and insignia of an American hospital inscribed on it. Lucy slit it open with great precision. It seemed to her that the very act of opening the letter was a sign of weakness. She felt she had acquiesced in Peter's remote plans. No doubt Peter, who did not think highly of the good sense of women in general and sisters in particular, would have instructed her to trust everything to his ambassador. In short she was to hand all their lives into the care of a flippant stranger. Miserable and mutinous, she unfolded the thin sheets and began to read.

It was much as she expected. Peter wrote with great affection but, as always, as if at least two-thirds of his mind were elsewhere. First of all he gave her a factual account of his symptoms which Lucy skipped without conscience. Then he commented unfavourably upon the spelling and handwriting of his offspring and attributed both to Lucy's own erratic habits in that direction. He added a terse criticism of the village school, which brought him to essentials. In two brief sentences, as Lucy noted in gathering wrath, he disposed of the children's future, consigning them together with their incompetent aunt to the care of Robert Challenger. He was her loving brother. That was all. Lucy searched in vain for any account of Robert Challenger. There was no description of him, no history, however lightly sketched. Above all there was no reason given for his election to the guardianship of the children. Who he was, or why he was judged suitable for that office, was ignored.

Lucy let the letter fall from her hands, torn between distress, annoyance, and a rueful half-desire to laugh. It was, of course, exactly the sort of letter Peter would write, indeed had always written. His infrequent epistles from school to their father had had just that ability to go straight to the heart of the matter. Comments upon the unvarying menu and the wildly various performances of the sports teams of which he was a member were invariably followed by crisp requests for such essentials as his piece of coral or his Mickey Mouse pencil-sharpener to be despatched with all speed.

She cast a disparaging look at his latest missive and cast it from her. In spite of her unwilling amusement she was disturbed. She began to move restlessly about the room, tidying magazines and plumping up cushions. It was all very well to laugh and in a way it was reassuring to know that Peter had not changed so much as might have been expected in the three years since she had last seen him. But these latest Olympian commands concerned more than his own well-ordered life.

Nervously, she took a cigarette from the rosewood box on the table. She seldom smoked and the cigarettes smelled stale. Lighting one with a spill from the fire, she made a face. She puffed jerkily for a few minutes, gagged on some particularly noxious lungful, and coughed, pitching the thing from her among the smouldering logs. Then she subsided into a chair, her head in her hands.

What was she to do? She looked uncertainly at the telephone. She could hardly telephone Peter at this hour of night. Indeed, she had no idea what the time might be in San Francisco, now she came to think of it. But certainly a trans-Atlantic connection would be beyond the scope of the evening relief staff at the rural exchange. And if she did telephone, always assuming she could discover the number of the hospital and Peter was available to talk to her and not asleep or on the operating table—what was she to say to him? He had always been more fluent than she was and would certainly have all his arguments ready to hand. Whereas she had nothing but a strong feeling of indignation at his cavalier treatment and a deep fear of the effect that his plans would have on the children, which was the most important thing of all, of course, and which she would find almost impossible to put into words. Particularly with a plausible and impatient Peter on the other end of a very expensive telephone line.

Lucy bit her lip. Where else could she go—for advice if nothing else? She had no doubt that her solicitor would corroborate what Robert Challenger had said. He was, she reflected angrily, by far too sure of himself to be mistaken on the subject. She began to nibble a finger-nail. Mrs. Browning would listen with enthusiastic sympathy, but there was nothing she could do. And as for Nicholas—Lucy sighed. Nicholas was a charming confidant when he had the time, but his advice was generally of an impractical nature. A great one himself for grand gestures without regard to the consequences or the people he offended by them, he had little patience with Lucy's more modest way of going to work. And at the moment, she thought wryly, he would not have the time even to listen.

She took her woes to bed with her and as a result hardly slept.

In the end she told nobody. For the rest of the week Colonel Browning kept her busy preparing the farm accounts. When she was not actually typing them out she was speeding about the farm collecting costings and production figures from the farm manager and his assistants. Mrs. Browning, who continued to pursue her plans for a Jacobean entertainment with unabated fervour, was a little put out to find her accustomed amanuensis so very thoroughly occupied. She even took her husband to task for overworking his secretary.

Lucy for her part was glad of the work. She even took the accounts home with her and pored over them when the children were in bed. Financially the farm was in a disastrous state. Until he had come to look at his affairs in the light of the new loan he was trying to raise Colonel Browning had not realised how very grave matters were. Lucy pitied him extremely. She flung herself into the fray, frequently working past midnight.

But however much her work might absorb her during waking hours she could not control her thoughts when she was, supposedly, resting. She spent countless hours, cold and wakeful, revolving in her mind various impossible alternatives. She could betake herself to the law, she might run away with the children. But the law was expensive and uncertain, and if she ran away somebody would be bound to find her. She was helpless and she knew it. She tried to be philosophical—perhaps the children *would* do better in boarding schools with others of their own age—but she knew too well how disturbed they were by the prolonged absence of their father and their mother's death to believe it. For both of them, Hazel Cottage and Lucy represented the only security they had ever found. It would be cruel to send them away.

58

And then she would fall into a light sleep full of night-mares of the children being persecuted and abandoned and would wake up, her heart thumping furiously with the panic of her dreams.

She grew noticeably haggard. By Friday evening her eyes were dark-rimmed with sleeplessness and her face looked pinched. Adelaide Browning was concerned. Coming into the farm office at three o'clock, she found Lucy sitting at the typewriter staring blankly before her.

'*Lucy*. My dear!' she exclaimed, hurrying forward. 'Whatever is it?'

'What?' Lucy was shaken out of her reverie. 'Oh, hullo, I'm sorry, I was miles away.'

'Outer Siberia, from the looks of it,' said Mrs. Browning shrewdly. 'You're not letting Tom's miseries get you down, I hope?'

'No, of course not,' she murmured, beginning to tidy the typed sheets beside her.

'Because you mustn't. Even if we have to sell the farm, life goes on. Though Tom doesn't believe it, I know. But he would be just as happy in a cottage growing his own cabbages. Farms are too mechanised nowadays. All the fun's gone out of them. So you mustn't be down-hearted about Tom.'

Lucy regarded her fondly. As she well knew, leaving the farm would be a major tragedy to Adelaide. 'I'm not,' she assured her.

Adelaide perched on the edge of her husband's desk. 'Then why the gloom? It's not like you. When I came in just now you had what my old grandmother would have called a face to fright the devil. Is it because you're overtired? Or just the October blues?'

'Both,' said Lucy uncommunicatively.

'What you need,' Adelaide informed her, 'is some fresh air. You don't get out enough.'

'It's hardly the weather for it,' pointed out Lucy, amused.

'Don't quibble. Air is air, even if it does come a little cold and damp at this time of year. Don't you ever go riding these days?'

Lucy sighed. While far from being an accomplished horsewoman she had taken great delight in riding occasionally. Before the children came to live with her she would often hire a horse for the day from the village riding stables and take a picnic on to the hill. Valerie Dale who ran the school was a childhood friend and sometimes she and her husband or Nicholas Browning would join Lucy. It had stopped with the advent of the children because neither of them could ride, and Lucy had soon found that to leave them for a whole day, even in the care of easygoing Mrs. Marshall at the farm, was to unsettle them for days.

'Have you stopped riding altogether?' Adelaide insisted.

'Oh well, I didn't really have time. And anyway, the stable is so busy nowadays, I'd be lucky if Val could lend me Brown Robin for more than an hour. And I wouldn't want to trot sedately over the bridle paths. When I go riding I like to get away.'

'Humph,' said Mrs. Browning, indicating dissatisfaction. 'Well, I don't care what you say. I think you ought to get out, for a couple of hours at least. I shall,' inspired, 'tell Nicholas to see to it.'

Lucy swallowed. It was in part a source of great comfort to her that Mrs. Browning was not aware of her foolish affection for her nephew. On the other hand it did occasionally give rise to rather painful situations.

'No, thank you,' said Lucy firmly.

'Oh, but that's just what you need,' Adelaide assured her. 'You'll never have the resolution to go down to the stables and ask Val yourself. Every time it occurs to you there will be just something you have to do first. Or else you'll be so tired you'll put it off till tomorrow. But if somebody else is coming with you—it's entirely different.' She spread her hands. 'Don't you see? If Nicholas were waiting for you, you'd *have* to go.'

'Yes indeed,' said Lucy with wry self-mockery. 'And that might be very inconvenient. Besides, hasn't it occurred to you that he might have other things to do? He might not even want to come riding with me.'

'Nonsense,' said Adelaide briskly. 'It'll do him good. He's been looking distinctly peaky. *I* think it's that new chef they've got at the Royal Oak. Have you seen him?'

Lucy shook her head. 'No. I met the waitress, though. Nicholas told me they came together. She's lovely. Is she his wife?'

'Good heavens, no. She's not really a waitress at all. She's an actress, Nicholas tells me. The new chef's sister, I believe. She was saying that she had just finished a summer season in some provincial theatre and couldn't get another job. Apparently it's always hard at this time of year. So she went looking for her brother to keep her, of course, and Nicholas takes her in.' Adelaide sighed. 'That boy has a heart of gold.'

Lucy looked at her incredulously. It seemed to her that even his fond aunt must have noticed that Nicholas was enchanted by his new employee. Adelaide returned her look defiantly.

'He just hasn't the heart to turn people away,' she added.

Lucy choked. 'Er—he did need a waitress,' she murmured. 'And she's very pretty.'

Adelaide sniffed. 'Not to my way of thinking. She's too thin and she hasn't got any eyebrows.'

Irresistibly, Lucy began to chuckle. Adelaide surveyed her for an offended moment before she too laughed.

'I know I'm a cat,' she said without obvious contrition. 'But she looks quite appalling.'

Essentially fair-minded, Lucy had to disagree. 'I thought she looked rather pretty,' she remarked. 'More than pretty.'

Adelaide snorted. 'Nonsense! She looks like one of those fairy tinsel dolls we put on top of the Christmas tree. They're just fancy wire if you take them to pieces. No substance to them.'

'Coo,' said Lucy. 'You really didn't like her, did you?'

Adelaide sighed. 'Oh, I'm fairly indifferent. Or I would be if Nicholas weren't such a *fool*.' She broke off and began to pleat her skirt absorbedly. 'We went there for dinner last night,' she continued, adding with a

61

flash of mischief, 'that's why my poor Tom has been like a bear with a sore head all day. He doesn't get on with Provençal cooking.'

'Then why did poor Tom agree to go?'

'Because I told him we had to or Nicholas would be offended,' said Adelaide fluently.

'Oh!' Lucy was taken aback.

'The truth is, of course, that I wanted to see her. My spies told me that there was the most ravishing waitress at the Royal Oak, so of course I wanted to go and see. Nicholas is *besotted*.' She brooded. 'But then he so often is, poor boy. And always with the most desperately un-suitable women.'

Lucy managed to smile. 'Well, be honest. Who in your opinion *would* be suitable for Nicholas?'

Adelaide shrugged pettishly. 'Oh, I don't know. Somebody he hasn't found yet, obviously. Not one of these sharp little town creatures he's so fond of. Somebody who knows about village life and the land and would be happy here.'

'Perhaps the new waitress is just a simple milkmaid underneath,' suggested Lucy with false cheerfulness. 'Wait and see. She may surprise you.'

'Don't be obstructive,' snapped Adelaide on a little spurt of temper. 'You know perfectly well what I mean. Men are such fools. He'd do much better with you.'

'I doubt it,' said Lucy with commendable equanimity. She looked at her watch. 'I don't want to hurry you, Adelaide, but I've got some things I must do before I go and meet the children. Did you want something special or did you just drop in for a chat?'

'Both,' said Mrs. Browning promptly.

Lucy fed paper into her typewriter and waited. 'Well?' she queried at length.

'It's a little difficult,' began Adelaide. 'You see, it's about this scheme of mine.'

'Oh yes?' Lucy was noncommittal.

'I know I said I didn't want you to do any of the organising, and I meant it—at the time.'

'At the time,' said Lucy hollowly. 'Yes. Only now you

do. What exactly do you want me to do?'

'Well, it's really that I want you to come and hold my hand while I do,' admitted Adelaide honestly.

Lucy stared at her.

'That beastly man at the Manor,' she explained. 'He's never there. And when I finally tracked him down on the phone he said I could go up tomorrow if I wanted, but he didn't sound very—welcoming.'

'He wouldn't,' said Lucy grimly.

'In fact he sounded positively hostile.' Adelaide looked at Lucy appealingly. 'Of course, I could go on my own. I mean, he's *asked* me—but I'd much rather have someone with me.'

'Me?' said Lucy in unfeigned horror. 'Oh, Adelaide, no!'

'But you've met him,' urged that lady, wheedling. 'You've talked to him.'

Lucy gave a short unamused laugh. 'Oh, I've talked to him all right,' she agreed. 'He is, without exception, the most detestable, arrogant, unfeeling man I've ever met!'

Adelaide blenched. 'Then you *can't* let me go and beard him on my own. It would be too unkind of you.'

'You're used to it,' said Lucy brutally. 'You have the knack of charming evil-tempered county councillors. Use the same technique on Mr. Challenger.'

'I don't think I dare,' said Adelaide frankly. 'He looks so very—' She sought in vain for a word.

'Unpleasant?' supplied Lucy.

Adelaide considered it. 'No, not unpleasant. I wouldn't have said he looked exactly *nasty*. We saw him at the Royal Oak last night, you know. He eats there every evening, apparently, and he was quite civil. It's just that he's a bit awe-inspiring. I think urban is the word I want. You know, one of those people that picks up the telephone and gets things done. The sort of man,' said Adelaide wistfully, 'that one doesn't say no to. I bet nobody ever keeps *him* waiting in all day for gas men who don't turn up.'

This was an old grievance and Lucy laughed. 'I think

that's a sort of Act of God, like earthquakes,' she said. 'I'm sure the Gas Board's no respecter of persons. Gas men don't turn up for everybody, all men are equal in their eyes.'

'Then he'd probably do the job himself,' averred Mrs. Browning. 'He looks that sort of man. Capable.'

'And stupid? No one in their right mind fiddles around with gas.' Lucy was exasperated. 'Oh, this is a silly conversation. I don't see why you can't go and see Mr. Challenger about this idea of yours without making up all sorts of gruesome stories about him to frighten yourself out of it.'

'That's because you have no imagination,' retorted Adelaide. 'If you could only see him as I see him you'd know why. He has an aura. I am very sensitive to people's auras.'

'In that case, why not write him a letter and not have to see him—er—aura to aura, at all?' demanded Lucy sensibly.

'Because then he'd say no,' said Mrs. Browning with simple truth. 'Oh, *please* come with me, Lucy. You needn't say anything. I'll do all the talking. But it would be such a relief to have someone with me. And you'd be ideal. You're so sensible. No matter how much you may dislike him, you're not in awe of him.'

She went to the door while Lucy watched her helplessly.

'I'll pick you up after lunch tomorrow. I really am very grateful. I know it sounds silly, but I really am quite frightened of him.'

The door closed gently behind her. Lucy sat and stared at it in dismay.

'And am I not?' she thought. 'God help me, am I not, too?'

CHAPTER IV

If Lucy had slept little during the last few nights she did not close her eyes at all that night. At half-past three she gave up the unequal struggle and went downstairs. The last few embers were glowing in the fire and she added another log to the powdery hearth and blew the cinders into a rudimentary flicker.

She made herself some hot chocolate and sat over the fire sipping this comforting brew and trying to make up her mind what she would say to Robert Challenger. He had promised to come and see her, she remembered, but he had not done so. Possibly her blatant hostility had persuaded him it would be useless. Perhaps he simply was not concerned with her at all. He could just drive up and carry the children off whenever he felt like it, thought Lucy, who always grew lachrymose in the small hours.

Yet something had to be said—even, she thought wryly, if only to concede defeat. It was inconceivable that she should invade his house in Adelaide Browning's train, listen meekly while that lady discoursed on Jacobean masques and heaven knows what else besides, and then simply leave without further reference to the children's welfare. She dwelled on the picture she conjured up for herself, and it filled her with embarrassed foreboding. She was nearly sure that it would inspire Robert Challenger with unholy amusement.

She gritted her teeth and tried to think of some way out of the tangle, but she was unsuccessful, and she eventually drifted into an uneasy sleep curled up on the hearthrug, one arm crooked on the seat of the armchair and her head bowed among its cushions.

It was in that position that the alarmed children discovered her the next morning.

'Lucy, Lucy!' gasped Boy, shaking her arm energetically. 'What's wrong?'

She stirred painfully, for her sleep had not been peaceful, and she awoke to a bitterly cold room and cramped limbs. But she was quick to sense their panic and to respond to it, even in her drowsy state.

'I couldn't remember whether I'd put the guard in front of the fire,' she lied, 'so I came down to see about it and fell asleep, that's all. What's the time?'

Angela was reassured. 'Late,' she said with satisfaction. 'We've been up ages.'

Boy, however, was still suspicious. 'Why didn't you put the guard up and go back to bed?' he demanded, swinging Lucy's hand roughly.

She blinked. 'Why—? Oh, I suppose I was just too tired. I just sat down and nodded off.'

'But why . . .' he began, but she interrupted him, her impatience only half simulated.

'Oh, please, Boy, forget it. It doesn't matter why. All that matters is that as a result of my own stupidity I've slept badly and you'll have your breakfast late.'

She stood up painfully. Boy let go her hand, scowling. Both children, who would normally have run off to the farm by this hour or gone down the lane to meet the postman, stayed very close to her. The kitchen was a large one and Lucy did not normally find it inconvenient, but, flanked by two small but determined sentries, she discovered it was not nearly as large as she had formerly thought.

At last, in desperation after breaking her second egg of the morning, she suggested, 'Why don't you go and sit by the window and tell me when the postman is coming?'

This activity amused them endlessly on days which were too wet for them to go outside and meet him. They usually had a competition for the first to make it to the kitchen to announce to Lucy his imminent arrival and the winner was allowed to pour Johnny Postman's tea into his own special red mug. He used to laugh and say that Lucy had never had his Saturday morning tea ready poured and waiting on the table for him until the children came to live with her. The children were proud of the office and would not normally have abandoned it. Angela indeed seemed half ready to take up her station in the window, but Boy vetoed it.

'No, thank you, Lucy,' he said politely. 'It's cold in the sitting room.'

Exasperated and a little worried, she did not try to persuade them. They ate their breakfast in near silence. Johnny Postman came, had his tea and commented upon their subdued faces, and left. Both of them refused to go out of the cottage although it was a bright clear day. They sat side by side in front of the fire, lit nearly two hours later than usual, doing a desultory jigsaw puzzle and bickering because they were bored. Lucy was too glad to be left alone to do her housework to complain, but as soon as the telephone rang they were at her elbow, peering anxiously at the receiver as if they could see there the portrait of the caller.

It was Adelaide Browning which seemed to relieve them and they fell away, going back to the fire and their squabbles.

'About this afternoon,' said Adelaide.

'Yes?' said Lucy with foreboding.

'Could we possibly take your car? The Mini's radiator has blown up and I hate driving the Land Rover.'

'All right,' said Lucy, sighing. 'What time?'

'As soon after lunch as possible. Before I lose my nerve.'

Lucy shuddered. 'Don't be so silly,' she said with unwonted sharpness. 'It won't be for some time. I got up late and I've been behindhand all morning. The children won't want lunch until two at the earliest. Say about half-past three. I'll come and pick you up.'

'Oh, very well,' said Adelaide, plainly not pleased. 'But don't blame me if we have to stay for tea.'

'Well, it will hardly be made of hemlock, if we do,' observed Lucy, preparing to put the telephone down.

Faintly from the other end of the wire came Mrs. Browning's parting shot. 'I wouldn't be too sure,' she said.

Slightly to Lucy's surprise the children were happy

enough to be left after lunch. They knew she was going out with Mrs. Browning and this was familiar enough to be unalarming. Boy went off to play with Billy Marshall and Lucy dropped Angela at the riding school on her way to the Brownings'. Both of them seemed to have recovered from the morning's upset, but they had been more disturbed by finding her downstairs than she would have expected, and she frowned. She cast a look in her driving mirror, but Angela was not standing waving at the gates but had hopped cheerfully inside with her friends without so much as a glance behind her. Lucy bit her lip. She felt she ought to be relieved at such resilience, but instead the children's very volatility was beginning to worry her.

She turned in at the gates of the home farm and stopped her old car in the drive. Taking the shortest route, she went through the office into the stableyard and across to the kitchen door. The house had been built as a dower house to serve the eighteenth-century squire's importunate mother-in-law whose shrill ghost was still supposed to haunt her sewing room. Since that date it had come down in the world and was now a somewhat rambling and untidy farmhouse. Lucy, who had known it since her childhood, loved it. Nevertheless she could see that it was becoming shabbier with every year that passed as Colonel Browning struggled to keep the estate together. The stables were empty now apart from the indigenous chickens which kept the Brownings and the Wilds supplied with eggs.

For a moment she stood looking round the empty yard. In the dark October afternoon it was bleak. She shivered.

'Lucy!'

She looked up at the imperative voice. Adelaide Browning was leaning out of an upstairs window.

'Don't stand there mooning. You'll freeze. Trot on, there's a good child.'

'Sorry,' she said, laughter suddenly lighting her eyes. 'Are you ready?'

'Yes, yes,' said Adelaide speciously. 'Just come up for a

moment, will you. I want your advice.'

'What about?' asked Lucy, standing her ground.

'Well, I'm not quite sure about this scarf,' began Adelaide, and broke off, hurt, as Lucy shook her head reprovingly.

'Come along, Adelaide. Courage!'

'I don't know what you mean,' began Mrs. Browning huffily, but Lucy interrupted her.

'Yes, you do. You're trying to put it off. I am *not* going to be lured indoors for a dressing-up session. You wanted to talk to the ogre. You've got an appointment. You've got a chauffeur. You can't chicken out now.'

'Oh, very well,' said Mrs. Browning, withdrawing her head from the window. 'You're a hard girl, Lucy Wild.'

In two minutes she appeared in the kitchen doorway, looking very elegant in a tailored suit with a bright scarf knotted audaciously at her throat. Lucy, who was wearing serviceable tweed trousers and a favourite soft lichen green sweater, suddenly felt dowdy.

'Oh well, let's go and get it over with,' said Adelaide. 'But I warn you, I'm terrified.'

Nobody, thought Lucy, would have guessed it. Still less would they have suspected it seeing Mrs. Browning greet her host serenely when she stepped out of Lucy's battered car not half an hour later.

She apologised prettily for bringing along an uninvited companion, explaining that her own car was out of commission and Lucy had been kind enough to offer her own, making it sound, thought Lucy resentfully, as if it had been her idea rather than Adelaide's. After one startled glance at her, Robert Challenger had seemed indifferent enough.

'But of course, you've already met Lucy,' said Adelaide, fishing delicately.

'Yes, of course. How do you do, Miss Wild? Won't you both come in? I'm afraid the house is still rather a junkyard, but there's a fire in the library. And that's really all that's needed to make a house habitable in this sort of weather, isn't it?'

69

They followed him, Adelaide chatting politely, Lucy silent. He held the library door open for them, giving Lucy a quick look as she passed him, half irritated, half amused. She affected not to notice.

As he had said the room was still only half furnished, with two large wooden chests standing against the window. He drew a chair, obviously swept clear of books and packages especially for Mrs. Browning's arrival, to the fire.

'Please sit down,' he said, looking vaguely round for another chair for Lucy.

She saw a little footstool beside the grate and sat on that. Seeing her choice, Robert Challenger looked relieved and leaned against the fine old marble mantelpiece, careless of the dust and paper shavings on it. His elbow, thought Lucy dispassionately, would be coated in dirt. She pitied whoever had to wash his sweaters.

'Well, Mrs. Browning, now that you've found me, what can I do for you?'

Adelaide was rather put out by this direct approach, Lucy observed. She would have preferred to pretend hers was merely a neighbourly visit before she plunged into the purpose of it.

'It's a little difficult to explain,' she began after a brief moment to collect herself. 'I don't suppose it will mean much to you unless you know anything of our local history.'

'Not a thing,' he said cheerfully.

'Oh. Well.' Adelaide looked desperately at Lucy for help.

It was not in her nature to refuse it. 'There's a Roman Way along the hill,' she explained quietly. 'At least there was. Now it runs through two fields which belong to a private company which refuses to admit a public right of way through them. We've fought it in the courts and gone as far as we could, but it would be very expensive to take it any higher. The obvious thing is to buy the fields in question.'

He nodded. 'I can see that. But what has that to do with me? I don't own any land on the hill, as far as I'm aware.'

Adelaide spoke again. 'Funds,' she pronounced.

'Ah, I see.' He was blatantly amused now. 'Of course, I shall be delighted to help.' He looked round the room again rather helplessly. 'When I can locate my cheque-book. It's here somewhere, I'm sure. I must ask—'

'Good heavens, we don't want *money*,' exclaimed Adelaide, quite shocked.

He stopped his search. '*Don't* want money?' He looked at Lucy. 'Then what the devil do you want?'

Adelaide looked flustered. 'Your house,' she said baldly.

'My *house*?'

Feeling rather superior—and very mean because of it—Lucy interposed quietly, 'Mrs. Browning thought that she might be able to raise money for the Roman Way appeal by giving a public entertainment here—as it's the oldest house in the village.'

'Here?' He looked round eloquently. 'Old it most certainly is, it's tumbling about our ears. But it's hardly Roman.' He looked at Adelaide, fascinated. 'What sort of entertainment?'

'Oh, something Jacobean, we thought,' she replied airily, basely suggesting Lucy's implicit support. 'A spot of singing—the Vicar conducts a rather good madrigal group. Perhaps the children might do a nativity play if it were at Christmas. The amateur dramatic society might care to do a scene or two from something suitable . . .'

Lucy, perceiving the gathering horror in his face, was hard put to it not to laugh. Adelaide did not observe it, and wove her fantasies on while he stood as if transfixed by the mantelpiece, unable to take his eyes off her.

'. . . and Lucy plays the lute,' she finished triumphantly.

Robert Challenger closed his eyes fleetingly, and the smallest perceptible shudder went through him. He opened them and glanced reproachfully at Lucy who, brimful of mischief, looked innocently back.

'Come now, Mr. Challenger,' Adelaide almost clasped her hands in supplication, 'what do you think?'

There was a slight pause while he seemed to be choosing his words.

'I think,' he said at length, carefully, 'it's a very—intriguing—idea. But as you can see'—he gestured largely—'there's hardly room for me here at the moment, let alone the school, the madrigal choir, the amateur dramatic society and the—er—public.'

Adelaide waved that aside. 'We'll all come and help you get the place ready,' she assured him. 'Of course. Won't we, Lucy?'

He began to look harassed. 'You're very kind, but I already have as much—indeed more—help than I can use. It's not just a matter of cleaning up and hanging curtains, you see. There's a good deal of structural alterations to be done.'

'Before Christmas?' demanded Adelaide keenly.

'Well, no, I suppose not.'

'Then there's no reason why we shouldn't use the house before Christmas, provided we put it in order, is there? I mean, we wouldn't be damaging your new decorations or anything.'

'I suppose not,' he said again.

The door opened and he turned to it eagerly, like a man reprieved.

'Ah, here comes that help I was talking about,' he said. 'I think she's been brewing tea. I do hope,' to Adelaide, 'that you drink tea. It's the only non-alcoholic beverage in the house.'

The door opened fully and a girl appeared at it, carrying a large and loaded tray. Robert Challenger went across to take it from her.

'There's no need for you to wait on me,' he protested. 'You do enough of that in your professional capacity.'

It was Simone Russell. Her pretty hair tied back at the nape of a slender neck with a bow and her cheek faintly dusty, she looked as if she had been helping very comprehensively with his housework.

'Thank you,' she said as he took the tray. 'Good afternoon, Mrs. Browning. Hullo, Lucy. I hope you also like ginger nuts. He's got absolutely nothing in his pantry except ginger nuts and potato crisps.'

She laughed at him with so much open affection that Adelaide, exchanging startled looks with Lucy, was quite confounded.

'Does Nicholas know you're here?' she inquired impulsively.

Simone looked surprised. 'I don't know. Does it matter? I don't start work until seven, you know.'

'Oh no. No, of course not,' murmured Adelaide. 'Forgive me.'

Challenger handed her tea. 'Simone's been over here a good deal,' he said with emphasis. 'She's really been very kind. I haven't been here all that much and she very kindly keeps a key and lets workmen into the place whenever I'm away.'

'You are fortunate,' said Adelaide, in measured tones, 'that she has such a very convenient job.'

He surveyed her with a good deal of comprehension. 'Aren't I?' he agreed gently.

Simone poured tea for Lucy and handed it to her. 'Oh, he's quite impossible,' she said with another laughing, intimate glance at their host. 'I never know when he's coming or going. He just disappears. This week, for instance, he suddenly took off. Then last night he appeared in the hotel for dinner without any warning. It's just as well he isn't married. No wife would stand for it.'

'No?' said Adelaide cattily, but Simone was impervious to insult. She looked like a little silken lapdog perched gracefully on the edge of a brimming piano stool. Her hair was quite as soft and shining as Lucy remembered it and her eyes were, if possible, larger. She had a low voice and a hurried, breathless way of speaking that made her sound like a solemn child. Her hands fluttered all the time she was talking, to the imminent danger of her tea cup and the papers on which she had set it. She was a fascinating little person. Nicholas at least, Lucy was gloomily sure, would not fail to be fascinated. Even in jeans and a dust-stained black shirt she had grace and a certain style.

Lucy averted her eyes in case she was caught staring—not that Simone would have noticed her regard or been in the least disturbed by it if she had. Simone, very obviously, had no eyes for anyone but her host. In his turn he treated her rather as if she were a child, petted and pretty, whom it amused him to indulge. He was very unlike poor Nicholas who looked quite foolish with love whenever Simone appeared. And his technique, thought Lucy viciously, seemed to have rather more success. Seeing Simone purring and preening herself beside him, Lucy was almost tempted to do something about it.

Adelaide meanwhile was trying to bring Robert Challenger back to the point. He had so nearly succumbed, she was sure, before Simone entered. She took him over the ground again very carefully.

Simone watched his face and seemed to only notice one word in ten of what was being said, but she did prick up her ears when she heard the word 'play'.

'Oh, are you going to do a play here?' she demanded artlessly. 'In the great hall?'

'Great hall!' scoffed its proud owner. 'Draughty great barn of a room. You could never heat it. The central heating won't be installed in the main house until the spring,' he explained to Adelaide triumphantly.

'Then we can use logs,' she replied with great serenity. 'That's what the Jacobeans must have used, after all. We've plenty of logs at the farm. You needn't worry on that score.'

'I won't,' he agreed. 'Mrs. Browning, are you serious? You've seen the sort of state the place is in. Even the kitchen isn't fitted properly yet. How can you possibly hold any sort of function here? It would be a farce!'

She looked at him and was struck by a brilliant idea. 'Of course,' she mused. 'I should have seen it before.'

'Seen what?' said Lucy uneasily from her chimney corner. She had seen that look before.

'A farce. When Mr. Challenger said that it would be a farce I saw at once what we ought to do. We must have a dance, a proper dance—you can see to all that, Lucy —but a *fancy dress* dance. We'll make people come dressed

74

as characters out of comedies. Oh, it will be charming!'

Simone nodded enthusiastically. Robert Challenger looked like one who has been struck down when he least expected it. Thinking of what Colonel Browning would say to this latest flight of fancy, Lucy shuddered. But Adelaide had found a fellow enthusiast and was not to be stopped.

'We can have the entertainment quite early in the evening—after all, the mothers will want to get the children to bed after the nativity play. How late are your two allowed up, Lucy?'

'Eight o'clock,' said their aunt mendaciously.

'Oh well, they'll just have to stay up a bit later for once. It'll be a treat for them,' said Adelaide dismissingly. 'But say they have to be in bed by ten. They could do their play at nine and then go home.'

'What time does the madrigal choir have to be in bed?' demanded Robert Challenger wickedly.

'Oh, they don't. They're grown up. They can,' said Mrs. Browning, paying him out nicely in all innocence, 'go on to the small hours.'

'It's to be hoped they won't, though.'

'They're quite good,' Lucy assured him solemnly. He drew a long patient breath. 'And it wouldn't matter if they weren't, becuase they're all related to half the county and all their friends and relations will come to hear them and pay good money into the Roman Way fund to do so,' she finished.

'You,' he said softly, looking down at her from his stance by the mantelpiece, 'are a very cynical young lady.'

'No, I'm not. Just practical. You want it to be a success, don't you?'

'Don't try my patience too far,' he warned. 'It's all very well for you to sit there looking demure. You know perfectly well I shan't be able to get out of it now. What a terrible woman!'

'Simone doesn't seem to agree with you,' she remarked.

Mrs. Browning and Miss Russell were already engaged in a spirited exchange of views on a suitable scene to be performed. Mrs. Browning had hitherto been the leading light of the amateur dramatic society, but it looked as if she would be so no longer. Lucy bit back a smile as they turned to Robert Challenger to adjudicate.

'*Twelfth Night*, or something more frivolous and eighteenth-century?' demanded Adelaide. 'What do you think, Mr. Challenger?'

For the first time he seemed really at a loss. 'I—really I—I wouldn't have an idea, Mrs. Browning. What do you think?' swinging round on Lucy sitting mumchance on her stool.

'Oh, eighteenth-century,' she assured them, with only the faintest tremor in her voice. 'Think what a beautiful age it was for dress. Nicholas would look lovely in a brocade waistcoat.' She paused and raised innocent eyes to Robert Challenger, as he towered over her. 'Perhaps you'll even be able to persuade our host to take part.'

There was a pause before Adelaide and Simone began to exclaim over the excellence of the idea. Lucy's victim meanwhile remained inscrutable.

Then he said, 'I can see I shall have to, as everyone else is going to. Nicholas, Simone, the Vicar—even your nephew and niece. And yourself, of course. I shall look forward to hearing you on the triangle.'

'Lute,' corrected Adelaide.

For one incredulous moment he stared at her and then his shoulders began to shake. 'Lute,' he said. 'Of course. How—how silly of me.'

Lucy, blushing furiously, glared at him.

'Only she never does play it for anybody,' complained Mrs. Browning.

'Well, she'll have to this time, won't she?'

Lucy stared at him. It was a joke, a dare, a piece of mischief, and yet he made it sound faintly threatening. Mr. Challenger it seemed did not care to be teased. She wondered briefly that Simone dared to treat him with such confident casualness. Then, before other disasters could strike, she left in Adelaide's wake, saying nothing more beyond a murmured goodbye—scuttling out, she thought disgustedly, like a beetle caught away from its stone. But she did not think she could outface him and, given that, she did not dare to stay.

All that afternoon Lucy chided herself for her cowardice. After all, they would have a good deal to say to one another if he was, however unjustly, to be the children's guardian. He had a right to expect her to discuss the subject with him. After so unsatisfactory an interview, he must surely seek her out. She did not look forward to it.

So when there was a knock at the door that evening, her heart jumped into her mouth. She told the children sharply to go and get ready for bed before she went to open the door. Puzzled and suspicious, they trailed after her, not quite disobedient but obeying her with the absolute minimum of zeal that just stopped short of defiance. Boy in particular trailed disconsolately upstairs with many an uneasy glance over his shoulder.

It was something of an anti-climax to find the doorstep full of Rusty with Nicholas Browning hovering apologetically in the shadows behind him.

Instantly the dog bounded in, to be met by Angela, all vestiges of obediences thrown to the winds, who leaped down the stairs to meet him. Lucy's greeting was more restrained. She patted Rusty's broad head and stood aside for Nicholas to come in.

'You're out at an unseasonable hour,' she observed, taking his coat from him. 'No customers tonight?'

'None that the others can't very well deal with on their own.' He ran a hand through his tousled hair. 'I suddenly felt I had to get out. The atmosphere was oppressive in the restaurant. The customers had got round to coffee and the place stank of cigars and cold food, and I just couldn't take any more. So I brought Rusty out for his walk early.'

Lucy raised her eyebrows but returned no comment. She led the way into the sitting room which, as always after an evening with the children, was in total disorder. Nicholas, a little bewildered, picked his way across a floor strewn with cushions and diminutive vehicles to the fire. He sat down, his hands hanging loosely between

77

his knees, staring absently before him. He looked tired and, Lucy thought, rather unhappy.

She went into the hall and quelled the children's romping. Ignoring their reproachful faces, she said firmly, 'Go upstairs and wash. You may come down and say goodnight in your dressing-gowns. But only,' with great emphasis, 'if you go up *now*.'

They went. Rusty padded after her and settled down at his master's feet, totally obscuring the fire. She hauled on his hindquarters—which, being an amiable beast, he did not appear to resent—until he was at right angles to his former position and seated herself opposite Nicholas. Rusty, quite happy as long as his nose remained in contact with Nicholas's shoes, gave a gusty sigh and closed his eyes. Lucy smiled.

'If only he were a fifth his present size that creature would be quite perfect,' she said.

Nicholas started. 'What? Oh, Rusty. Yes, he's a good soul.'

And he went off into his sorrowful reverie again.

Lucy sat quietly with her hands in her lap waiting for him to speak. She was not embarrassed by his silence, for she had known him too long. It was, besides, a rare pleasure to see him seated at her fireside, for he seldom left the Royal Oak in the evenings. For a moment, half ashamed, she played with the fantasy that they might be man and wife, the children upstairs their own, the whole of Sunday stretching peacefully before them. For a moment the picture was so strong—and so attractive —that she almost reached out to take his hand. Then he looked up and she drew back, blushing.

'What am I going to do, Lucy?' he said wretchedly. 'I'm in the most frightful mess, and it's all my own fault.'

Lucy clasped her hands strongly together and wished that he did not appeal to her quite so much.

'Most of the really bad messes usually are one's own fault,' she said dispassionately. 'What have you done—or not done—this time?'

For a moment she thought he wasn't going to answer her, and then he sprang up and went to the window.

Rusty, dispossessed, growled, then sank his head on to his forepaws and slept again.

'I'm in love, Lucy,' Nicholas burst out. 'This time it's for real. And she—'

'She—?' prompted Lucy painfully.

'Oh, she's quite kind to me. She lets me tease her and take her out occasionally. But she doesn't really know it's me. It could be anyone—most of the time it is. She's so attractive, everyone wants her.' He laughed bitterly. 'Every time the telephone goes now it's one of her men. And she treats us all the same.' He smote his fist against the palm of his hand. 'I won't have it. It's not good enough. She must take me seriously. But what can I do? It's better to be one among many than not to have her at all.'

'Is it?' said Lucy, really intrigued. 'I mean, doesn't your pride revolt?'

'Pride? What pride? I haven't any pride left. I haven't had for weeks. As soon as I saw her—' He stopped, biting his lip. 'I'm sorry, Lucy, I didn't mean to come and harangue you.'

'Didn't you?' she said dryly.

'Well, yes, I suppose I did. I feel you're the only one I can talk to about her.'

'I take it that these agonies are in connection with Simone Russell?'

He flushed. 'There's no need to be sarcastic. Just because you're so phlegmatic yourself, that's no excuse to laugh at other people.'

'I'm not laughing at you,' she denied. 'God forbid! I just like to have my facts clear.'

Nicholas glared at her and then, slowly, relaxed his tense pose and came back to the fire. He took her hand.

'Oh, Lucy, you're good for me. You always make me laugh.'

'Thank you,' she said ironically. 'Well, so the lady is Simone. You're in love with her, you see her every day. There are a couple of rivals waiting to be swept from the board. I don't see the difficulty. I would have thought you were in a very strong position.'

'She doesn't notice me,' he insisted. 'I'm just there to light her cigarettes and open doors for her as far as she's concerned.'

'And pay her salary,' Lucy pointed out.

He shrugged. 'Well, yes, and pay her salary, I suppose. Perhaps that's what's wrong. Perhaps if she worked for Challenger, instead of just seeing him now and then . . .'

'Challenger?'

'The new man who's bought the Manor. I thought you knew him—Adelaide told me you did. Anyway, it's not important. The only important thing is that Simone is crazy about him. She spends all her free time up at his house. He never takes her out, he just lets her slave away for him up there—and she goes like a lamb. He exploits her and she can't see it. He just lets her hang around because she's useful, but he'll forget her easily enough when he goes away. And she thinks he'll take her up to London, help her find a job . . .' He broke off, exasperated.

'She sounds a little—er—gullible,' observed Lucy. She found her fingers crooking into talons and straightened them hastily. 'He's hardly a theatrical agent.'

'No, but he's rich and sophisticated and she says he has contacts. Contacts!' He flung his hands up to his brow despairingly. 'She's such an innocent.'

'She's certainly an optimist,' agreed Lucy equivocally. 'Have you tried hinting that he might not be quite such a safe bet as she imagines?'

'Hinting! I've told her in so many words. But she doesn't believe me. He thinks she's the greatest thing since Sarah Bernhardt, according to her. He's devoted to her, he just hasn't the time to devote to her at the moment.' He sighed. 'Unless he goes away permanently or produces an alternative object of devotion, Simone just won't believe any wrong of him.'

Lucy looked thoughtful. 'You mean unless he transfers his affection elsewhere?'

'Or brings one of his sophisticated London girl-friends down here.'

'He'd hardly be so obliging as to do that.'

80

'No,' Nicholas said gloomily. 'No, he wouldn't, would he? So there's no hope.'

As always Lucy found herself torn between irritation and a helpless desire to take the whole sorry mess out of his hands and deal with it herself. She looked at him lovingly. He was pale and dishevelled and he looked very young. An idea, dazzling in its simplicity, terrifying in its danger, took shape. A small smile, which Nicholas did not observe, began to curl the corner of her mouth.

'No hope?' she murmured. 'Oh, I wouldn't say that.'

CHAPTER V

Although Lucy fully expected a further visit from him Robert Challenger did not in fact put in an appearance at the cottage in the ensuing week. Instead, Lucy had a rather severe letter from her solicitor, announcing that Mr. Challenger had been to see him and he was fully satisfied that he was her brother's proper representative during his absence from the country. In a handwritten postscript, he congratulated Lucy on now having a man to turn to to resolve the problems necessarily attendant upon the care of children. Lucy flung the letter into the fire in a fit of temper.

She was too busy to brood upon it, however. Her every free moment—and a good few when she was supposed to be working for Colonel Browning—were occupied by what Mrs. Browning had come to call her Masque.

Lucy had to go into Newbury to fetch ten copies of the Restoration play selected by the Amateur Dramatic Society and then spent two evenings faithfully transcribing in pencil into each copy Mrs. Browning's amendations. Mrs. Browning had abridged it in order to produce an intelligible performance of no more than forty minutes' duration. The result, Lucy felt, was not happy as Mrs. Browning had been unable to bring herself to cut out any of her own major speeches or materially to reduce the number of scenes. Those charged with changing the scenery would, as far as Lucy could see, be on the stage quite as much as the actors. However, she kept her reservations to herself and even went along to the first rehearsal in a friendly spirit, to prompt and make tea in the interval.

Jane Frobisher had volunteered to write the nativity play, which fortunately consisted mainly of exclamations of surprise and admiration, and Lucy was typing this scene by scene as it arrived.

But her most important duty, as Mrs. Browning earnestly assured her, was to see to the Manor itself and make sure that they were not the tiniest, littlest bit of a nuisance to Mr. Challenger. With a heavy heart she promised to do her best.

Obviously the first thing to do was to clean the hall in which the festivities were designed to take place. She could not remember precisely how large it was, but, judging from the appearance of the rest of the house, was reasonably certain it would be filled to capacity. From Mrs. Appleton's day, when she had been a frequent visitor, she could recall a cold, high-ceilinged apartment. When she was a child it had reminded her of nothing so much as a cathedral. There had been an enormous refectory table in the middle of it, she remembered, on which had always stood an enormous bowl of whatever flowers were in season. Probably both table and bowl were still there, begrimed with ten years' dust and surrounded by the new owner's possessions. She would have to telephone and ask his permission to make a start.

When she did so, Simone answered the phone. She seemed disappointed to hear a girl's voice, but was friendly enough and even offered to help in what she acknowledged would be a mammoth task. Lucy thanked her.

So, as soon as Colonel Browning could spare her from the office, she donned jeans and an old shirt, piled the car with brooms and mops and every imaginable detergent, and set off about her task.

When she arrived it was to discover Robert Challenger's unmistakable car sitting in front of the house. She looked at it with dislike. It embodied everything she most detested: it looked fast and disreputable and most unsafe. Just like the man, she thought, scowling horribly.

'It's only a poor piece of machinery,' said a voice laughingly.

She jumped and turned round to find Robert Challenger standing in the doorway. Feeling transparent, and annoyed at being caught hating his car, she glared at him.

83

'What?' she snapped.

He strolled over and patted the bonnet gently. 'This simple object which arouses your ire. It's merely a machine. Quite inoffensive.'

'Except when someone's inside it,' she flashed.

'Have you still not forgiven me for your little scuffle in the ditch? That was quite your own fault, you know. You mustn't take it out on the car.' He chuckled. 'You looked as if you might kick the poor thing just now.'

'I'm not so childish. I don't kick things.'

'I'm relieved to hear it.' He took a fistful of brooms from her car. 'I see you came prepared. Simone's already at work. Shall we go in?'

Somebody had already done a great deal of work in the hall, she found. Most of the heavy furniture had been pushed into the centre of the room, and the crumbling velvet curtains had been pulled down. They now lay in a heap by the window, with Simone mourning over them.

'They must have been so beautiful,' she explained. 'Really rich.'

Lucy surveyed the ruins. 'As far as I remember they were a rather depressing shade of dark prune,' she said dampeningly. 'And they were old and tatty even when I was a child. I'm surprised they're still in one piece.'

Robert Challenger fingered them disparagingly. 'They're not,' he said. 'They're just held together by moth-holes. I suppose I shall have to have some more made. How tedious! I never thought moving into a house would be so time-consuming.'

'Let me help,' offered Simone eagerly.

He looked amused. 'What can you do, little one? Sit up all night, sewing curtains by candlelight?'

She was crestfallen. 'No. But I could help you choose the colour . . .'

'Ah, that I can do for myself,' he said. 'It's practical help I need.'

'I would have said,' remarked Lucy fairly, 'that Simone has been of very great practical help to you so far.'

He was wearing his darkened glasses again today and

they made his expression at that moment unreadable. Nevertheless, she had the impression that he was laughing at something private and altogether hidden from her and Simone. It annoyed her intensely.

'Would you?' he said. 'I suppose you're right. I haven't really been sufficiently grateful. I'm sorry, Simone. Forgive me.'

'Of course. And anyway, I'm happy to help.'

'So what about the curtains?' demanded Lucy. 'You wouldn't have needed them, at any rate not just at once, if it hadn't been for the Masque. So—if you like to buy your material—I'll make them up for you. That seems a reasonable division of labour.'

He seemed startled. 'You? But will you have time?'

She shrugged. 'I have time for anything provided I make it.' She grinned suddenly. 'It will get me out of the dramatic society rehearsals, anyway, if I say I have to stay home and sew their curtains. It will be worth it.'

'Don't you like acting, Lucy?' asked Simone, beginning to push the curtains out of the way and ply her broom.

'Not very much,' said Lucy with restraint. 'Anyway, I can't.'

'Nonsense,' said her host. 'It's just a matter of getting dressed up and showing off. All women like it.'

And having thus offended both his listeners he went off to fetch the rest of the cleaning implements from Lucy's car.

They worked more or less in silence until it was nearly dark. Simone kept saying that she ought to return to the Royal Oak and downed tools presumably with that object. But she continued to sit on the table swinging her legs and making helpful comments long after she had done so. At last the exasperated Lucy was about to ask Robert Challenger to take her away when they heard a voice outside and Nicholas appeared.

'Hullo,' said Robert Challenger, apparently unsurprised. 'I didn't hear a car.'

'I walked,' said Nicholas briefly.

'Oh, did you come through the churchyard?' inquired

Lucy, leaning on her broom. 'I wondered if the old gate was still there.'

'It's there, it's just overgrown. In fact it's nearly rusted away. I pushed my way through quite easily. The path on the other side is waist-high with nettles, though.'

'We used to go through the orchard down to the river by that gate,' said Lucy dreamily. 'We were trespassing, of course, but Mrs. Appleton never minded. We used to take picnics down to the stepping stones. Do you remember, Nicholas?'

'Yes.' The monosyllable was very nearly rude. 'Are you going to be long, Simone?'

She moved reluctantly. 'I should have left ages ago. It's only—that is, I was wondering—do you really not want some help choosing curtains, Robert darling?'

Nicholas looked hurt and Lucy found she was gripping the broom so tightly that the handle was causing a red weal across her palms.

Robert Challenger tipped her chin with a long forefinger. 'Do you think you could help me, pussycat?' he teased.

Lucy interrupted. 'You'll need to take measurements,' she said prosaically, 'and make sure you get the right weight, if you want velvet again. I'd better come with you.'

There was a pause. Nicholas looked shocked as if she had somehow betrayed him and gone over to the enemy, she thought despairingly, instead of trying to help. She glanced at Simone and was shocked in her turn. For once the sweet expression was entirely missing. The girl was glaring at her with undisguised venom. But that was not what shocked Lucy. It was rather the calculating and altogether adult look of spite that had crept into Simone's eyes, wholly at variance with her usual kittenish expression. Lucy's broom fell with a crash.

Robert Challenger picked it up courteously. 'That's very kind of you. I'll accept, if I may. When will you be free?'

'The sooner the better,' said Lucy sturdily. 'As it's for

the Masque, Colonel Browning will give me a morning off. Tomorrow?'

'Excellent. But make it the afternoon, we shall have more time. And perhaps I'll be able to persuade you to extend the expedition to have dinner with me.'

Lucy protested. It was impossible. There were the children to be collected from school, given their dinner, put to bed.

'I'm sure Simone will be glad to meet them and feed them,' he said with a mockery which made Lucy feel momentarily sorry for the girl. 'She's such a helpful little thing.'

'I wouldn't dream ...' began Lucy, but Nicholas interrupted.

'Of course you must go. I can meet the children and I can leave them with Adelaide until you get back. I don't suppose you'll be terribly late. She'll be delighted. And even if she isn't,' he said undutifully, 'it's a small thing to do for this crazy idea of hers. She seems to have set everyone else by the ears. Let her take a little of her own medicine.'

'I don't think I like hearing my niece and nephew referred to as if they were a dose of salts!'

'Don't carp,' said Nicholas with the astringency of long acquaintance. 'Just thank God for an evening away from them and go.'

Lucy was about to resist when she glanced again at Simone's tense, furious face. She lifted her chin. 'Very well,' she said, sounding as if she were going into battle, 'I will. And *you*,' to Nicholas, 'can tell Adelaide that you volunteered her as a babysitter. Because I won't.'

But Adelaide was charmed. The children would be no trouble. They could help carry books down to the church hall. She despatched Lucy with her blessing in Robert Challenger's rakish car.

For most of the afternoon the conversation was severely practical, for which Lucy was thankful. She still had the uneasy feeling that, behind the dark glasses that he still wore, her companion was laughing at her. She mistrusted him and deeply resented Peter thrusting him upon her as guide and mentor. It was as if Peter had no confidence in her. Which, she thought, sighing, she supposed he didn't. Like Nicholas, he had never realised that she had grown up. Her mouth quirked wryly; grown up and grown old, she thought, in comparison with Simone.

'What are you smiling at?' he asked.

'My thoughts.'

'Amusing?'

'No, not really. Just that it's ironic that Peter should still think of me as an irresponsible child.'

'Why?'

She turned amazed eyes on him. 'Why? Can't you see? Because I'm neither, though I sometimes think I'd like to be. I'm old and settled and boring. If anything I'm too old to have charge of the children, not too young.'

'You're a complete baby,' he said calmly, and turned the conversation into other channels.

They did not return to personalities again until they were sitting opposite one another at the dinner table. It was early and they were very nearly alone in the restaurant. Lucy had been regaling Robert with some anecdote about the Brownings which he had seemed to find entertaining when she suddenly became aware that the quality of his attention had changed. She trailed off into confused silence.

'And you looked like a complete fool,' he said, repeating some words of hers thoughtfully. 'It's very important to you, isn't it, what other people think of you?'

'Not unduly,' she defended herself. 'Only some people.'

'Like Nicholas Browning?'

'Him among others,' she said quietly. 'My friends.'

He seemed obscurely angry. 'Friends! Parasites. You let people batten on you. You even encourage them to do so. Peter, Nicholas, his mad aunt. You don't owe them anything. Why do you let them run your life?'

'I wasn't aware that I did.'

'Oh, nonsense. You must know it. You run around

after the Brownings like their personal scullerymaid. Why, for God's sake? This isn't the eighteenth century and they're not lords of the manor.'

Lucy made a helpless gesture. 'I love them,' she said simply.

'Love!' he scoffed. 'You just lie down at their feet and say "Walk on me" and they do. You should take a firm stand. Make up your mind what you'll do to earn a living wage and don't get involved with them beyond that.'

'How?'

'Oh, lord, how should I know how? You just learn by experience. Haven't you acquired any defences at all in your life?'

'I haven't learned to stand aloof from people I care for,' she said haughtily. 'I don't know that I'd care to learn.'

He slapped his hand down on the table. 'Then you're a lost cause,' he snapped.

But it seemed it was a subject he did not want to leave alone and when he finally delivered her to the cottage and saw her inside he did not, as she expected, immediately take his leave but stood leaning against the kitchen table, surveying her.

'Do you know what Peter told me about you?' he demanded.

'Something not very flattering.'

'He thought it was flattering.'

Lucy began to busy herself with the percolator, assuming that he was staying for coffee unasked. He took her elbow and turned her gently round to face him.

'Don't you want to know?'

She shook her head. 'You make it sound too terrible.'

'He said you were a quiet little thing. I gathered you had no mind or will of your own and weren't too bright into the bargain.'

She chuckled, 'I can believe it!'

'Yes, but you mustn't believe it,' he said urgently. 'It's a stupid image that these people here have of you and you mustn't let them convince you it's true.'

89

Lucy backed away from his confining arm. He disconcerted her. She had found his half-mocking friendliness enlivening but difficult to deal with. This new seriousness quite bewildered her. On the one hand she resented his assumption that he had the right to speculate on her private life. On the other, she found his obvious sincerity a little alarming. It was a breathtaking experience to find oneself suddenly the object of somebody else's whole attention. One she was not used to.

'I don't think,' she said gently, 'that you know me well enough to pass judgement.'

'Oh yes, I do,' he contradicted, his mouth suddenly bitter. 'I know you very well indeed. Much better than your neighbours. I'm the one you ground to powder beneath your chariot wheels over the children, remember?' He gave an unamused laugh. 'Peter hadn't bargained for that.'

'No,' she agreed. She looked at him silently. 'Do you expect me to apologise?'

'Good God, no! You were perfectly right. I'd have done the same thing, I expect. The only thing I don't understand is why you suddenly changed tack and from being furious, suddenly began to wonder if Peter was right and you weren't good for the children.'

Her eyes widened. 'How did you know that I did?'

'I told you, I know you very well.'

'But you don't.' She put her hands to her cheeks. 'You can't. I mean, we've hardly met. Have you been spying on me?'

'No more than you have on me.'

Lucy blushed. 'Oh, gossip,' she said dismissingly. 'It doesn't *tell* you anything. I don't know anything about you. For instance, I don't even know why you wear those ridiculous glasses. Unless it's to make you look more like a film star and fascinate poor Simone,' she added unwisely.

There was a nasty silence, unbroken except for the bubbling of the coffee. Then Robert said slowly, 'Did I say you had no defences?'

'Not against people I *love*,' she emphasised. 'And you

were right—I don't need them against people I love.'

'Like Nicholas Browning,' he nodded. He was no longer laughing. 'You're a sharp-tongued and head-strong harridan. If you want to know about my glasses you have only to ask. Or no, I'll tell you. You know I'm an engineer. There was an accident with some explosive, and my eyes were damaged.'

She drew a shaky breath and began muttering, 'I'm sorry, I didn't know . . .'

'No, but you could have found out, couldn't you? Instead of concocting malicious fantasies.'

'I've said I'm sorry,' she began with dignity, and gasped as he suddenly snapped the light off. 'What . . .?'

'Since you disapprove of my dark glasses,' he said blandly, 'I'll take them off. Unfortunately I can't stand strong light yet. You'll simply have to make coffee in the dark.'

'Oh, don't be childish,' she said crossly. 'I'm not playing games at this hour of night . . .'

'Are you not, by God?' he snapped, and pulled her roughly into his arms.

Her peevish protests were silenced by his mouth. He was angry, but there was more than anger in it. It was almost as if he were himself shaken by his own urgency to have her in his arms. Lucy, her rib-cage half crushed and her head dancing, put up no more than a token resist-ance. It was strange, it was exhilarating, it was deeply undignified. She abandoned herself to the new sensation. She closed her eyes and ran her fingers pleasurably through his crisp hair. He drew a little ragged breath and put her away from him.

'And all because Nicholas Browning's bit of fluff can't make up her mind,' he said cruelly. 'You're quite a crusader, Lucy Wild.'

She stared up at him bemused. Her fingers plucked convulsively at the stuff of his jacket. She found, to her chagrin, that she did not want to be put aside in that controlled way. It was insulting. He had no right to make her feel warm and alive as if she had never felt either in her life before and then push her away. Lucy reached up and touched his cheek softly.

Robert retreated as if stung. He caught her hand and held it against his face in a hard clasp for a moment before throwing it furiously from him.

'You,' he said unevenly, 'want to learn to look after yourself before you try looking after Nicholas Browning. That coffee is boiling.'

And he was gone.

He left her shaken and oddly ashamed of herself. Quite what she had done or said to offend him she could not recall. Yet she had the uncomfortable suspicion that he had been quite serious in his overtures of friendship and she had, by her own clumsiness, repulsed him almost without meaning to do so. It was very lowering.

She collected Angela in a chastened frame of mind and listened unresponsively to the little girl's chatter. Apparently they had taken the ponies along by the river and the riding instructress had shown them how to sit still on a horse's back while it was drinking. Angela, one of the expert few, had not fallen off even once.

'Well done,' said Lucy absently.

Angela was disappointed. Mrs. Browning had been far more impressed. She had not quite dared to recount her triumph to Colonel Browning, but she had confided in Boy, who had been disparaging. Boy had little time for horses and none at all for any occupation that did not appeal to his wayward sense of adventure.

In fact Boy was in disgrace. He had climbed on to the stable roof whence he would no doubt have withdrawn in his own good time if by an unlucky chance Colonel Browning had not happened to see him. The Colonel had been setting off on his evening stroll with the dogs which usually took him past the Royal Oak. He had instantly commanded Boy to descend, reprimanded him sharply for risking his neck, and then taken him off with the small party of retrievers and spaniels to, as he put it, take the young devil out of Adelaide's way.

Lucy wondered whether Angela, who was devoted to the dogs, might not resent this favouritism. But she was afraid of the Colonel and did not envy Boy his outing in the least.

The Colonel returned Boy, both of them in high fettle in spite of the Colonel's well publicised aversion to children, well after any acceptable bedtime. Boy, who was aware of this, eyed Lucy cautiously. His experience of his aunt's discipline was such as to lead him to expect retribution to fall once his adult champion quitted the house. But such was not the case. Lucy was distraite. She hardly seemed to notice the time. Beyond one searching question as to whether he was tired—which he hotly denied—she seemed most uncharacteristically willing to let the matter slide. Surprised and relieved, he went off to bed whistling.

In the following days the children found that their aunt was more and more absent-minded. She was very busy, of course. But she had been busy before without forgetting where she had put their school books when she tidied up or allowing them to stay up hours after curfew without a murmur. Sometimes they would find her staring into space doing nothing.

They did not understand it but on the whole were inclined to be grateful for the resulting relaxation in her normal vigilance. They were very fond of Lucy. She was tolerant and lighthearted and always interested in what they were doing. But she was a little more careful of their well-being than was generally considered quite proper among their contemporaries. They were not allowed to cross the main road without an adult in attendance, for example, or to go splashing through the river with the Marshall children after little trout. Not that the Marshalls ever caught anything, but they covered themselves finely in mud and river slime and clearly had a very good time. Boy had long since given up begging to join them on these expeditions, although they were goodnaturedly willing to have him along, but he now began to wonder if he might not slip away from Lucy's slackened grasp and take part in their amusement.

Therefore, on the next fine Saturday afternoon, when Lucy was sewing, Boy and Angela crept out of the house.

Lucy's sewing machine was an old one, and she would not have heard the kitchen door close above its clattering anyway, but Boy felt it was more suitable to the nature of the enterprise if they went on tiptoe, their wellington boots in their hands. He closed the door behind them with exaggerated care and they were off down the lane as fast as they could run. They would go through the churchyard and through the hedge that bounded it, down to the stepping stones from which the Marshalls conducted their nefarious sport. With a little luck—as long as Angela did not get over-excited or fall in—Lucy might never find out about it.

Certainly Lucy, sitting amidst a sea of deep blue velvet curtaining, had her mind very far from her niece and nephew. Adelaide Browning, who had expressed surprise and a certain displeasure when informed that Lucy had offered to make the curtains for the hall at Windrush Manor, was intending to visit the cottage for a consultation. This meant that she would regale Lucy with a list of complaints against the other actors in the play, rehearse her lines, accept tea and leave. In passing she would probably delegate a few more tiresome and time-consuming jobs to Lucy. Already she was charged with procuring and delivering costumes and appropriate lighting to the Manor. Fortunately the district fire officer had vetoed the use of candles at a public performance which had been Adelaide's first wish. In place of them Mrs. Browning fancied an array of fairy lights. No doubt, thought Lucy tiredly, they were to be hired from somewhere. She would simply have to discover a name. When she had pointed out to Adelaide that all this took time and that precious commodity was rapidly running out, her only reply had been, 'I knew you were doing too much. You should never have agreed to make those curtains.'

Today she arrived brimming with the enthusiasm of newly-learned speeches and a new idea. It had occurred to her that the hall was flagged, cold and very sparsely furnished. Why not fill it with conifers? The trees would have to be cut for Christmas anyway, as the Colonel always presented each family in his employ with a Christmas tree. Why not have them felled ten days early and, threaded with coloured lights, use them to decorate the Manor. Wouldn't it be pretty?

'How many?' asked Lucy indistinctly, breaking cotton with her teeth and drawing out a long line of even tacking stitches.

'Oh, a dozen or so. The hall is big enough.'

'Undoubtedly,' agreed Lucy. 'But am I? How big do you expect these trees to be?'

'Oh, a good size. Ten or twelve feet at the least.'

'Lord,' said Lucy devoutly. 'What would we stand them in?'

But Mrs. Browning had no patience with such trivialities. 'Oh, flowerpots,' she said vaguely. 'You'll find something.' She fingered one of the completed curtains that Lucy had let fall to the floor. 'You know, this velvet is rather charming. Was it expensive?'

Lucy shrugged. 'I wasn't paying. I didn't look.'

'It's nice. And so is the lining. I suppose that's one of those synthetic fabrics. I must say it's a lovely colour. The man has good taste. Or did you help him choose it?'

'No,' snapped Lucy. 'They're his curtains. He's got to live with them. They're nothing to do with me.'

'There's no need to bite my head off,' returned Adelaide in mild surprise. 'It's just one of those things one doesn't quite imagine men doing, that's all.'

'He's emancipated,' said Lucy between her teeth.

Adelaide chuckled. 'He is indeed. Do you think he'll stay at the Manor? He hardly seems a *likely* inhabitant, if you know what I mean.'

'You mean he hasn't applied to join the madrigal group?'

Adelaide giggled. 'He wasn't very civil about that, was he? I don't know what right he has to be so superior. I bet *he* can't sing for toffee. He'll have to get dressed up, though,' she added with slightly malicious satisfaction. 'Everyone is. Even poor Tom.'

'Good God,' said Lucy, startled. 'What on earth—'

'Oh, nothing too terrible,' Adelaide assured her.

'He wouldn't stand for it,' she added wistfully. 'He's going to wear hunting pink and be Jorrocks.'

Lucy swallowed. 'Er—does he know?' she inquired delicately.

'Not quite. Not yet.' His wife looked wise. 'At the moment I'm holding velvet breeches and a brocade waistcoat over his head. He'll be so relieved that I've given that idea up that he'll wear almost anything. But I'll tell him in my own good time.'

'It's hardly Jacobean,' observed Lucy.

'No. We've thought of that at the Committee. We discussed it and decided that a sort of village fancy dress was the best idea. Then those in the play can come in their costumes and the children can all be dressed as angels or whatever and the people who buy tickets can come as what they like.'

'Talking of tickets, have you actually sold any yet?'

'Well yes, I have, as a matter of fact.' Mrs. Browning looked pleased with herself. 'I wasn't even trying either. Tom's bank manager dropped round last night and actually *asked* for some. I had to write them out by hand. I did wonder if you'd get some printed and—oh, open a ledger or something. You'll know what to do.'

'But I don't think I shall have time,' objected Lucy, startled.

'You can always make time for what you want to do,' said Mrs. Browning sententiously, looking hard at the curtains.

'No, really, Adelaide. I'll get the tickets printed with pleasure, but you'll have to get someone else to sell them. You'll need posters too, by the way.'

'I've thought of that,' said Mrs. Browning loftily. 'Jane is getting the children to do them and then blocking in the relevant information herself. I gave her the office telephone number, by the way, as a sort of box office, so I'm afraid that whoever answers the phone has to sell the tickets. I didn't realise you wouldn't want to.'

'It isn't that,' said Lucy, bowing to *force majeure*. 'I was just hoping to fit a little of the farm work round this project of yours. But I can see I shan't manage it.'

96

'Tom won't mind,' said Adelaide blithely, her spirits restored. 'I've told him it's just until Christmas. Anyway, it must be a relief for you to do something other than those boring old accounts all day.'

'I don't do accounts all day,' said Lucy, put out. She enjoyed her work.

'Well, paying dreary bills and reading awful advertisements for machines, then,' amended Mrs. Browning. 'At least my ideas have some life in them.'

'Yes, I suppose so,' murmured Lucy, abandoning any attempt to convince Adelaide of the interest in the farm's office work. Adelaide loved her house and the farm, but its organisation baffled her and any attempt by her husband to explain its finances to her threw her into a frenzy. She simply could not grasp that to Lucy it was as absorbing as her local charities were to her.

Now she was looking at Lucy a little pityingly, head on one side. 'You don't sound too bright. Think of something jolly. What are you going to wear?'

'Wear? Me? When?' said Lucy, lost.

'To my fancy dress affair, of course,' said Adelaide impatiently. 'You'll have to come dressed up as something.'

'Oh no! Do I really have to? After all, I shall be helping . . .'

'And playing the lute,' said Adelaide.

Lucy was silent.

'Well?'

'Adelaide, I'd much rather not. You know—I've refused to play for the Vicar's group so often, I'd feel mean if I suddenly agreed to play for you. And I'm really not very good.'

'Nor is anybody else,' said Adelaide unanswerably. 'Don't be a snob.'

Lucy laughed. 'I'm not a snob. I'm—'

'Shy?'

'Yes, I suppose so, if that's the way you want to put it. I don't want to impose my excruciating performance on the unsuspecting.'

'Nobody who comes to any binge of *mine*,' said Adelaide

blandly, 'is unsuspecting.'

Lucy laughed suddenly. 'You mean they'll have asked for what's coming to them? Oh, very well, I suppose I'll play. But only one piece. And I won't be able to dress up. A lute isn't small, you know. It's bigger than a guitar. I can't manage a farthingale and all the trimmings as well.'

'Then you'll have to change,' said Adelaide calmly. '*I* think you ought to go as the Home Farm ghost.'

'What, the shrill mother-in-law? Delicious!'

'She wasn't all that old, by our standards. Not much over forty. And there's a lovely portrait of her when she was a girl.'

'*Is* there? I've never seen it.'

'Haven't you? It's in the old nursery. She's got a gorgeous pink dress on, all floating ribbons and lace.' Adelaide looked thoughtful. 'You're clever with your needle. Why don't you try and make a copy of it? It needn't be expensive. You could even use stuff like that lining material,' she went on, warming to her theme. 'And I've got some old lace . . .'

'Adelaide, I haven't got *time!*' almost wailed Lucy.

Mrs. Browning sniffed. 'You know, Lucy, you're middle-aged before your time. When I was your age I was out dancing every night until three or four o'clock and up at eight the next morning to go to work.'

Lucy sighed. 'I haven't your stamina,' she acknowledged, snapping off the final thread. 'There, that's the last. I can take them up to the Manor tomorrow . . .'

'No need,' said Adelaide, looking out of the window. 'He must be a warlock. Here he comes.'

'Comes? Who?'

'The lord of the manor,' she replied mischievously. 'Well, go and meet him. He looks in a mood to batter the door down.'

He did and he was. Lucy opened the door in some trepidation to find Robert in the act of raising a furious hand to the door knocker. She flinched and retreated.

'Yes?' she said faintly, remembering their last encounter and blushing.

He did not appear to notice.

'You,' he said, 'are the most amazingly careless, criminally stupid woman I've ever met.'

Lucy blinked. 'I—I'm sorry?'

'So you should be,' he said savagely. 'So you will be if anything like this happens again.'

'Anything like what?' she demanded, quite bewildered.

'Letting those children run around on their own,' he said, with a wide gesture. Behind him two weary and woeful figures began to toil up the path as if its slight gradient were the north face of Mont Blanc. Lucy's heart went out to them, they looked so very chastened. She went down on her knees and took them into her arms while Robert looked down at her bitterly. 'I suppose you didn't even know where they were.'

The injustice of this for a moment held her speechless. She opened her lips to retort, saw that Angela was on the verge of tears, and held her peace. She stood up, one small hand held firmly in each of hers. 'No, I didn't, as a matter of fact,' she said calmly. 'I apologise if they've been trespassing again.'

'Trespassing!' he snorted. 'They were indeed. On the stepping stones. They could have fallen in easily and no one would have known what had become of them.'

Lucy paled.

Boy spoke up at this manifest inaccuracy. 'Yes, they would,' he objected, albeit in a thin voice. 'Billy or Rob Marshall would have known. And Angela or me. We wouldn't *all* have fallen in.'

'Perhaps not,' said Robert Challenger, moderating his tone somewhat. 'But could Billy and Rob have pulled you out if you *had* fallen in?'

Boy considered this, his fingers twitching in Lucy's comforting clasp. 'N-no,' he acceded at length.

Unexpectedly Robert Challenger smiled. 'Good. Remember that. And don't do it again.'

For a brief second he regarded Lucy unflatteringly. He was wearing his dark glasses and she quailed. His masked face looked remote and unassailable, and her explanations died on her lips. Like a judge out of a nightmare he looked cold and accusing. The children felt it and huddled against her.

'Don't you do it again either,' he said to Lucy distantly. 'Or I really will do something about it.'

She lifted her chin at the threat, but, very conscious of the clinging children, still said nothing. Adelaide, unable to contain her curiosity any longer, came out into the hall and stood behind her. She could hardly have heard what he said, but his tone was unmistakable. And if she had not heard it, Lucy's attitude of brave defiance would have told her everything anyway.

She came forward, trying to ease the situation, saying gently and pleasantly, 'Have Angela and Boy disgraced you, Lucy?'

'No,' said Lucy, head high, looking Robert Challenger straight in those hidden eyes. 'No, not at all.'

He drew a quick angry breath. 'And I suppose you'll let them off and forget all about it?'

'That,' she said with perilous calm, 'is my business.' She was shaking with reaction—loud voices always overset her—and she knew she was not far from tears herself.

'That,' he said silkily, 'is a matter of opinion.'

Once again Adelaide tried to come to her rescue. 'I really don't think you can say that, Mr. Challenger. Lucy is responsible for the children after all.'

'She is indeed.'

'If they've damaged your property, I'm sure they'll apologise,' poor Adelaide ploughed on. 'You can't blame Lucy. It's not easy for a woman to bring up two children of that age on her own.'

He turned blank glasses on her. 'No?' he said politely. 'Then perhaps they need a father figure to take them over?' And he turned on his heel.

CHAPTER VI

As soon as he had left, a shaken Adelaide drew the children indoors to the fire. They were cold and muddy, but the damp that clung to their clothes seemed to emanate more from the foggy atmosphere than any truant acquaintance with the river waters. Lucy followed them indoors, shaking.

The unpleasant little scene had made her feel physically sick. She could tell from Adelaide's quick, deprecating glance that it showed in her face. Briskly, or as briskly as she was able, she commanded the children to discard their clothes and bath. Without a word, they obeyed.

Once they were splashing in the bath their spirits were soon restored and Lucy could hear them giggling. She went into the kitchen and began to heat milk.

Adelaide followed her. 'Phew!' she exclaimed. 'He doesn't mince his words, does he?'

'No,' returned Lucy briefly.

'Is there anything I can do?' Adelaide looked round the kitchen. 'Cut bread for toast, or something?'

Lucy roused herself from her panic-induced torpor. 'That would be kind—thank you. Only don't toast it. They'll want soldiers, I expect.'

'Soldiers?' queried Adelaide, finding the bread and investigating a drawer for the bread knife.

'Marmite soldiers. Didn't you have them as a child? You cut the bread into long thin strips and smear the Marmite on fairly thinly.'

'Oh, those. Yes, of course. Nicholas used to have them as a little chap when he came to stay with us. I remember it used to infuriate Tom. It was just after the war when everything was scarce and he used to say he couldn't bear to see good food being shredded. I never saw his objection myself. At least it meant that Nicholas would *eat* it. Most of the time he refused to eat. I've never known such a difficult child. At least you haven't had that trouble with Boy and Angela.'

'No,' said Lucy with an effort. 'No, that isn't a problem of theirs or mine.'

Whoever would have thought that he could be so brutally rude? She had recognised from the first that he would make a powerful adversary and that was why she had treated him so warily. But she had never envisaged such a blighting direct attack. Her mouth shook. Aware of it, she turned away from Adelaide. He had always seemed casual, careless even. Now that it was manifestly clear that he was neither, what would he do? Sweep the children off to their reluctant grandparents? Banish Boy to prep school and Angela to heaven knows where? How could she defend them from what she was rapidly coming to believe was inevitable? How could she explain to them?

She took a jar of chocolate powder from the top shelf and began to stir a spoonful into the steaming milk. Adelaide watched her from the corner of her eye. She looked very pale. Of course she had always been a sensitive little creature, easily dismayed by her father's boisterous tempers. He and Peter had done all they could to moderate their behaviour to reassure her, but they had not always succeeded and Adelaide had not infrequently found the motherless child sobbing in some forgotten corner. She had always hoped that Lucy would outgrow her extreme sensibility. Over the years she had certainly learned to disguise it. Few people now, knowing her as an habitually self-possessed woman, would credit the shrinking child that Adelaide suspected lurked behind the façade. Really, she was unduly and quite unnecessarily distressed by Robert Challenger's outburst.

'It's ironic that he should catch the children doing the very thing you've forbidden them to do on the one day they get away from you. I mean, they're usually so good.'

'Yes,' agreed Lucy dispiritedly. After her initial

indignation she had lost all desire to defend herself. She had just wanted him to go away and leave them in peace. Besides, from his point of view he was justified. From any point of view, she supposed. She *had* been careless. They should never have been allowed the opportunity to escape to the river.

Adelaide put an arm round her shoulders. 'Now you're not going to worry about what that overbearing man said, are you? After all, it's nothing to do with him.'

Lucy gave a long shudder. 'They could have drowned,' she said, releasing the thought uppermost in her mind.

'Nonsense. They could have got very inconveniently wet, but even that is highly unlikely. Children have a very healthy sense of self-preservation. None of the Marshall brood have ever drowned or even fallen in, as far as I know.'

'But they're older and bigger and they've lived here all their lives. Angela's so little . . .' She broke off sharply.

'Is that any reason to spend your time foreseeing unlikely disasters? She'll grow. And come to no more harm than most children. Try for a little philosophy.'

Lucy stirred the chocolate absently. 'It's not easy to be philosophical with other people's children.'

'All the more reason to try. Otherwise you'll stifle the poor things.'

'Oh, lord,' said Lucy, torn between laughter and tears, 'you too!'

And, declining to explain this remark, she set out a tray for the children's supper and carried it in front of the fire.

She fully expected to hear or see more of Robert Challenger once his temper cooled and he decided what steps were to be taken. She braced herself for another meeting with what courage she could muster. The children found her loving as ever, but a little withdrawn. It took more to capture her interest, unimaginably more to make her smile than hitherto. They did not quite understand but were somewhat impressed by her changed aspect. Connecting it dimly with their earth-shaking escapade they behaved with exemplary obedience.

When no word came from Robert Challenger Lucy became, if anything, more alarmed. She could not rid herself of the feeling that they had passed some crisis in their relationship and that he would no longer allow her custody of the children to go unchallenged. And on the following Friday morning the blow fell.

A letter from Peter's solicitor announced that Boy was to go away to school. He would start at the local cathedral choir school in January. He was very lucky to get a place in the middle of the academic year, the letter pointed out, and she would no doubt wish to thank Mr. Robert Challenger, himself an old pupil, to whose good offices this fortune was due.

Lucy quailed. Boy's saintly behaviour had not escaped her notice and she thought she knew the reason for it. He knew he had offended and was afraid, not of punishment, but of her displeasure. To be sent away to school would seem like banishment to him. Over break-fast she tried tactfully to suggest that he might find it interesting to go somewhere else to school and detected the quick flare of panic in his eyes. She abandoned the subject and took the children to school.

If only, she thought, walking back down the lane in a biting wind, they were not so like me. If only they didn't worry so much about being abandoned. Or if only I didn't know they were worrying. I shall have to put a stop to this, but I can't imagine how.

She was sitting in the office trying to pluck up courage to telephone Robert Challenger when Adelaide Browning walked in.

'Good morning,' she said brightly, 'I've got some-thing for you.'

'So,' said Lucy, as she was supposed to. 'Something nice?'

'Come and see.'

Lucy did her best to shake off her dismal air. Adelaide was plainly pleased with herself and it would be churlish to spoil her fun. Besides, if she were honest, she was glad of an excuse to postpone her telephone call. Obediently she rose and followed her mentor.

They went across the house, heads down against the gale, and upstairs to the top storey. Here the servants had once been housed, but their draughty attics had long since been turned into bedrooms. Adelaide passed these, however, and went to the long studio at the far end of the corridor which had been the nursery. Lucy had memories of playing with Nicholas in there. It had been rather a grand apartment, clearly designed for a number of children far in excess of the two that was all the household could muster by that time. She and Nicholas had been a little overawed by it. They would sit in the middle of the circular rug, she remembered, playing cautiously with the wooden soldiers which had been Colonel Browning's, always glad when it was teatime and they were called downstairs.

'I haven't been up here for years,' she remarked, looking round her.

'Nor has anyone else, by the look of it.' Adelaide ran a disgusted finger along the dust on the banisters. 'Oh well, I suppose it doesn't matter. Mrs. Shepherd doesn't have time to dust everywhere. It doesn't look as if we'll have any use for the nursery for some considerable time. Unless Nicholas marries this Simone child.'

She opened the door and led the way in.

'Do you think he will?' asked Lucy painfully. One of the more horrible aspects of her present predicament was that she could not go and discuss the ogre's tactics with Nicholas. In his present state of absorption she felt it would be an intrusion.

'I doubt it. She's after Challenger and makes no bones about it,' said Adelaide with crudity but sound practical sense. She threw up a couple of blinds from the deep windows and looked round. 'There!'

Lucy, on the threshold, could see why she and Nicholas had found it so uncomfortable a playroom in their youth. The walls were hung with family portraits and an enormous grandfather clock dominated one end of the room. The other was filled with a large mantelpiece and bookcases to the ceiling.

She drew a long breath. 'Now there's a chimney for Father Christmas to come down,' she observed. 'The children are getting very restive about the size of the one at Hazel Cottage. They're sure he'll get stuck.' She walked across to it. 'Good heavens, Adelaide, it must be nearly four feet deep!'

But Adelaide had not brought her to the nursery to admire its architecture. She turned her round to face the wall opposite the windows. 'There,' she said again.

Lucy peered in vain. She seemed to be addressing herself to four very dingy portraits, three of gentlemen in breeches and—a slight gleam of dirty yellow in the pervasive murk—lace ruffles, one of a lady.

'Oh, look,' said Adelaide impatiently. 'Isn't that the most divine dress?'

'I can't see it,' confessed Lucy, feeling a failure.

'Well, it is a little difficult to make out just at first, but look *hard*.'

Thus adjured, she did her best but could perceive nothing more than a grey wig of indeterminate shape and what she took to be a hooped skirt. Despairing, Adelaide led her up to the painting and began to outline the details.

'Look, it's got a low neck, there, with lace down the front, and a little lace frill round her throat . . .'

'Like a garter,' exclaimed Lucy, successfully perceiving it.

Adelaide was put out. 'It's very pretty,' she said severely. 'And very romantic. See, the dress must have been satin. It's striped in two shades of pink and it has a sheen to it . . .'

But that strained Lucy's credibility too far and she fell away. 'I'm sure you're right,' she said hastily, 'but I simply can't see it.'

'You're not looking properly,' Adelaide reprimanded her.

'No, very likely not. Though I'm sure it's lovely. But why the excitement? Have you suddenly discovered it's a Reynolds or something?'

Adelaide snorted. 'It's to be your dress for the Ball.'

'Oh, it's a full scale Ball, is it now?'

'Eventually,' said Adelaide with composure. 'I always intended it should be.'

'How devious,' said Lucy admiringly.

'Don't try to flatter me, and *don't* think you can side-track me, because you can't. That is your dress. If you won't make it up I shall do it myself. It's about time you had something pretty. Tweed trousers and twin sets,' muttered Adelaide. 'Anyone would think you were my age. It's not good enough.'

'I try to look what I am,' said Lucy, half amused, half offended. 'I wouldn't want to appear any different.'

'Then you should.'

'What's wrong with the way I look?'

'Everything,' said Adelaide comprehensively. 'You fade into the background. Oh, it's admirable for a farm secretary, I'm sure, but you're not a farm secretary every waking hour of your life. You always look—dependable,' she produced, a little cruelly. 'Dependable and unobtrusive.'

'Oh dear,' said Lucy.

'It's all very well in its way, but you could do with a bit of variety. Learn to frivol a little. And *that* is why I want you to make that dress.'

'It's certainly a garment to frivol in,' agreed Lucy, peering once again at dimly discernible flounces. 'But is such a metamorphosis really necessary? I mean, can't I just buy something new . . .' She trailed off before Adelaide's grim expression. 'No, I can see I can't. But why do you suddenly want to dress me up, Adelaide? It's never happened before,' she pointed out shrewdly.

Mrs. Browning bit her lip. 'To give that little vixen a run for her money,' she said frankly.

Lucy was momentarily bewildered. 'Little . . .? Oh, you mean Simone Russell. What's she been doing, Adelaide? Upstaging you?'

'She ruins my best lines,' agreed that lady calmly. 'But it's not that. I don't like this—fascination—she seems to have for Nicholas. She treats him like a tame animal. I think she ought to be shown that she's not the only—'

'Lion-tamer?' supplied Lucy, seeing her lost for a word. 'No, really, Adelaide, I can't try to vamp Nicholas. For one thing, I've known him too long and he'd see through it. For another thing, I wouldn't care to. He probably wouldn't notice anyway,' she added gloomily.

'He doesn't have to,' Adelaide assured her. 'Just as long as she does. Nothing like a dash of healthy competition.'

'It sounds distinctly unhealthy to me,' complained Lucy. 'I can't plot over Nicholas, like this. You can't expect me to.'

Adelaide was taken aback by her agitation. She stared at her. Lucy blushed.

Then, patting her arm, Adelaide said, 'Very well, my dear, if that's how you feel. You don't have to talk to Nicholas at all if you don't want to. But *do* make this dress. It's quite delicious.'

'Adelaide, I *can't*. I can't even see it. All I can make out is a vague notion of lace and ribbons. I would have to have a more detailed original before I could make a copy.'

'Get a book out of the library,' said Adelaide. 'Or no, better still, come and look at my porcelain figures. They'll give you a real three-dimensional pattern to copy. Come along. They're in my bedroom.'

Unprotesting, Lucy followed. It was obvious that she was not to be let off. It might even, she allowed, be amusing. She liked sewing. It soothed her and she thought wryly that she would be grateful for some soothing occupation in the next few fraught weeks. She therefore inspected Adelaide's figurines with more than simple admiration.

There were four, two pairs. One was a flirtatious pastoral pair, the shepherdess improbably attired in a full, panniered gown with tiny rosebuds garlanded about her. The other pair were larger, more impressive pieces, the gentleman in stiff court brocade, the lady equally grand.

'They're beautiful,' said Lucy, turning this last in her hands.

Adelaide made a face. 'And horribly valuable. The insurance is staggering. *And* I have to keep them locked up in that loathsome cabinet, which I hate. I think I ought to sell them sometimes. God knows, we could do with the money. But I don't like to think of them going into a museum with lots of other poor creatures caged in a bigger and better cabinet. Perhaps I'll give them to you,' she added, inspired.

Lucy was startled. 'Good heavens, what an idea! The children would almost certainly chip them. And anyway, if you can't afford the insurance, do you imagine I can?'

'I suppose not.' Adelaide sighed and took the court lady from her. 'I do hate this slavery to financial institutions that we have to endure. And I don't suppose anyone would insure against two schoolchildren.' She dusted her sleeve across the little figure. 'I suppose you're coming to look on them as permanent residents.'

Lucy did not answer immediately. Adelaide looked at her unobtrusively. She was certainly not looking well recently. Now her face was pale, making the dark shadows under her eyes all the more obvious. Plainly her recent preoccupation was due to more than the imminence of Adelaide's plans coming to fruition. Plainly too she did not want to talk about it.

Now she seemed to give herself a little shake and say with an effort at humour, 'You suppose a good deal, Adelaide.'

'Well, aren't you?' insisted that lady.

'Thinking of them as permanencies?' Lucy sighed. 'I don't know what to think. I haven't heard from Peter except—' she bit it off. She was very fond of Adelaide, but she found she did not want to confide in her that Peter was reluctant to entrust his children to her care. 'Anyway, he won't be home *this* Christmas,' she went on hurriedly.'

'Oh dear! Will the children be terribly disappointed?'

'They're becoming philosophical. Boy hoped that Peter would make it for his birthday. When he didn't—

well, they were both rather low for some time. But now I think they're resigned. After all, they haven't seen him for a year.'

'It's a long time at that age,' observed Mrs. Browning sagely.

'It's a long time at any age,' retorted Lucy.

'Well yes, but . . . Do you think they've forgotten him?'

She shook her head decisively. 'Not in the least. They're just living for Daddy to come home. It's rather terrible. And I aid and abet them in a way. I can always put them off by saying "Wait and see what Daddy says". Angela wants a dog, for instance. She loves dogs and she is always hanging around Rusty, which I don't like because he is much too big and rough for her. But I don't actually get her a puppy because I'm not sure whether Peter would like it.'

'But Peter wouldn't mind,' said Adelaide, puzzled. 'He was always very fond of animals.'

'Yes, I know. But if he comes home in the spring and wants to take them off on his travels with him he won't want to take a dog as well. And even if he did, he couldn't then bring it back into the country without it going into quarantine for ages. Not only is it inconvenient, it's extremely expensive.'

'So poor Angela doesn't get her puppy?'

'She hasn't so far,' admitted Lucy, 'Though I don't think I can hold out much longer. If nothing unexpected happens I may give her one for Christmas,' she said with sudden decision.

The simplicity of the scheme took her breath away. Let him try separating Angela from a new pet. And let him try to unload that new pet on to her grandmother along with the little girl and he would get very short shrift. Elaine's mother was a quiet, determined lady who had run a conspicuously ordered home for thirty years and more. Although she might be foolish enough to overlook the havoc that two healthy children could cause, she would not be blind to a puppy's capabilities in that direction. Lucy began to smile. She must find some way to let him know that she had decided to welcome a puppy into Hazel Cottage. If it did not precisely spike his guns it would at any rate serve to show him that she was not going to submit without resistance.

'Yes, that's a very good idea. In fact the more I think of it, the more sensible it seems. I was wondering about Christmas presents. That will answer very well for Angela.'

'Where will you get the pup?' demanded Adelaide practically.

'Oh lord, I haven't got round to that yet. I've only just decided. Wherever there's one available, I suppose. I'd rather have it from someone I know than from a pet shop. I'll ask around. Someone in the snug at the Royal Oak is bound to know of one somewhere.'

'Ring Nicholas up now,' suggested Adelaide enthusiastically.

But Lucy declined. 'No, thank you,' she said, not quite disguising her recoil soon enough. 'I'll be down there soon, I expect. In the meantime, if you want me to make up this dress, I shall have to ask you to lend me some paper and a pencil. It shouldn't be too difficult, I think. But I'll just make a sketch in case I forget anything.'

The next weeks were fully occupied. Lucy typed and duplicated and delivered and collected all day, and sewed her own and the children's costumes most evenings. One of Nicholas's customers found her a golden retriever puppy for Angela, but otherwise her Christmas shopping was neglected.

The children, however, were more conscientious and their bedrooms became suddenly and mysteriously full of scraps of cardboard, shavings of what looked like wallpaper, and all polished surfaces of their desks and chests acquired a coating of crystallised glue. Lucy, the best of aunts, coaxed this last off uncomplainingly and did not so much as peer into their cupboards to discover the secret.

In all this time she did not encounter Robert

Challenger except casually once or twice. He was always in a group of people whenever she caught sight of him at the Royal Oak and at any other time invariably had Simone at his elbow. Knowing she was a coward, Lucy was nevertheless glad to avoid a tête-à-tête. He had written to her once, briefly, when she had objected to the solicitor that there were not sufficient funds to cover Boy's fees at this new school that his guardian had appointed. Robert Challenger had sent her two curt lines stating that he was responsible for the fees until such time as the trust fund for the children was set up. Lucy had seethed with the desire to tell him that she did not require his charity. Only the absolute conviction that he would point out that it was nothing to do with her what he spent on his wards had restrained her from confronting him.

Nevertheless it was a subject on which she continued to feel strongly. On the couple of occasions he had come on her unawares he had surprised a look of such venom in her expression when she caught sight of him that he could be in no doubt of her feelings. He had not referred to it, however, although he did tease her one evening for sulking in her chimney corner when she refused to join him on a trip to the local cinema with Simone and her brother. Lucy had been annoyed, but she had shrugged it off. Nicholas, who was looking drawn, clearly approved of her decision. Robert Challenger, infuriatingly, looked as if he found it amusing. But he did not try to persuade her.

She did not see him again until the day of the Ball. She had gone dutifully into the farm office to find Colonel Browning with his feet on his desk and a mulish expression on his face.

'I am not,' he announced before she had said a word, 'moving from here until lunchtime. I know Adelaide thinks I'm going to run around after her committee, but she's wrong.'

And he advanced a large nature magazine in front of his nose defiantly.

'I'll tell her,' said Lucy, laughing. 'I take it I'm to be

seconded to her today?'

Colonel Browning waved a hand. 'Yes, of course. Better go and find her. It's been bedlam! She kept waking me up last night and making me write things down on the bedside notepad. I don't think she closed her eyes.' He pondered gloomily. 'Come to that, I don't think I did. She didn't let me.'

'I'd better see what I can do,' said Lucy, going. 'Er—perhaps you'd be better for a snooze.'

'Huh! What hope have I of a snooze in this madhouse today?'

'You could always walk down and see Nicholas,' she suggested mischievously.

'What's that? Nicholas? Lord yes, so I could.' His feet came off the desk with a crash. 'You're a good girl, Lucy,' he informed her. 'Got initiative. I like that. You'll make someone a good wife. Got sympathy too.'

But she was already half way across the yard and gave no sign of hearing him.

Adelaide was not in as great a flap as Lucy had expected.

'Of course I shall have to rest this afternoon,' she told her importantly, 'or I shall be dead this evening. But I've made lists of everything that has to be done and there shouldn't be any last-minute crises.'

This sanguine belief proved unfounded. Lucy arrived at the Manor to find Robert Challenger struggling in the arms of a gigantic Christmas tree.

'What on earth—?' she cried, jumping out of the Land Rover which had been assigned to her for the duration of the campaign. She ran over to him and seized hold of a couple of stout lower branches and righted the thing.

'Thank you,' he spluttered, emerging. 'It suddenly seemed to develop a mind of its own.' He held it upright at arm's length, surveying it ruefully. 'It's the last and the smallest. The men have put up all the others. I thought I'd make myself useful and take this one in for them.' He ran a hand through his hair. 'Ugh! I'm stuck over with pine needles like a green porcupine!'

Lucy withdrew her steadying hand from the now stationary tree.

'I can see you are. What on earth possessed you to try to move it on your own?'

'I was doing all right until it began to wobble,' he said ingenuously. He looked at it with a good deal of satisfaction. 'I must say it's a fine specimen. I haven't had a Christmas tree as good as this in all my life.'

'I'm glad you're enjoying it,' said Lucy, her lips beginning to twitch in spite of her aversion to the man. 'I quite expected to find you in hysterics.'

'Did you? Do I look the hysterical type?' he inquired, interested.

'N-no,' she allowed, chuckling. 'But Adelaide's plans are enough to shake the strongest nerves. Her husband has retreated to the pub.'

'Sensible fellow,' Robert remarked, settling the tree lovingly against the side of the house and beginning to dust himself down. 'But I'm not going to follow his example. I'm enjoying myself. It's like a Marx Brothers film in there. The men from the farm are stuffing as many trees round the walls as they can get. It looks like the Amazon jungle. And now a couple of electricians are trying to festoon them with lights. Trees, not men,' he added, taking her elbow. 'You must come and join in. There's some lady from the committee spraying everything—indeed everyone who's so unwise as to stand still for a minute—with instant snow from a can. And of course the electricians, swinging from branch to branch like a couple of gibbons, are worth seeing. This way.'

Quite overcome, Lucy followed him into the hall. He had not understated the case. Picking her way among lopped branches, piles of holly left to scratch the unwary passer-by, and a tangle of wires and cable, she was grateful for his guiding hand.

'Careful,' he said, swinging her neatly out of the way of Mrs. Frobisher. The lady, oblivious, continued on her way with an air of determination, looking as if she were hot on the tail of an errant wasp. An uneven set of white splashes appeared in her wake and a good deal of the snow substitute was finding its way on to chairs and rugs. Appalled, Lucy looked at her host.

'Rather fetching, isn't it?' he said serenely, not releasing her. 'But *not* in the eye, I think. She really doesn't seem to notice where she's going, does she? Perhaps we ought to wear protective goggles or something.' He led her through the conglomerate mess to one of the long windows and sat her down on the window seat. 'Is this just a courtesy call, or have you come to add your mite?'

Lucy looked up at him. 'It's awful,' she sighed. 'What have we done to your home?'

He smiled a little crookedly. 'It's not a home yet. Perhaps this baptism of fire will make it one. Anyway, it doesn't matter, and if it did, it's not your fault. Don't look so guilty.'

'I can't help it. And I've got a hamper of costumes, and a tea urn and—oh, heaven knows what in the Land Rover that I ought to unload somewhere.'

He laughed. 'Well, that doesn't sound insuperable. The tea urn goes into the kitchen, and the hamper upstairs. Mrs. Browning decided it would be best to set aside a couple of rooms as dressing rooms. I'll show you and take the hamper up. Have you brought your instrument, by the way?'

Lucy shuddered visibly. 'No.'

His eyes lit with laughter, but he returned no comment beyond a murmured, 'Very wise!'

Thinking how much friendlier and altogether less alarming he looked without his glasses, she asked, 'Are your eyes better?' Then she remembered the last time they had discussed the subject and blushed furiously.

It was obvious from the way he looked at her that he also remembered the incident, and with some amusement. He primmed his mouth. 'Yes, thank you,' he said politely. 'I hardly need my glasses at all now. Although I still can't stand too much electric light,' he added wickedly.

Aware of being teased, Lucy raised her chin. 'That must be very inconvenient.'

Robert stood up, resting one foot on the window seat, his elbow on his knee and his chin on his hand. From this superior position he considered her. Lucy felt her colour rise and stared back at him indignantly.

'Oh, I wouldn't say *inconvenient*,' he drawled.

She saw no reason why he should continue to enjoy himself at her expense.

'Then let's go and get that hamper,' she said briskly. 'If you can stand the light of day.'

As she led the way out of the hall she could hear him laughing softly.

CHAPTER VII

The evening was damp and bitterly cold. Lucy, collecting the children early from school at the behest of Jane Frobisher, was sharply reminded of the approaching shortest day. It was dark by three and a cold mist rolled down from the hills. The inside of the Land Rover which she was still using was bleak and smelled of engine oil and damp leather—none of which could subduc the children's enthusiasm.

Both of them were featuring in the Vicar's nativity play. Jane Frobisher, who was nothing if not just, had carefully inscribed a part for every one of her pupils whatever their age, sex or condition. As a result she had, after carefully extracting potential angels, Virgins and monarchs, a rather motley collection of shepherds. Billy Marshall, who was their chief spokesman, had drilled them like a sergeant-major so that, once grouped on the stage, they uttered their devotions and expressions of surprise with a military precision which threatened Lucy's gravity severely. So far she had preserved a respectful expression at such rehearsals as she had attended, but regarded the evening performance with some trepidation. Fortunately, the children would not at all mind if she laughed—they did it themselves frequently enough, after all. However, Lucy could well imagine such a proceeding giving great offence to Mrs. Marshall and other proud mothers and was determined to sit right at the back of the hall during the performance, whence she could flee precipitately if her feelings threatened to overcome her.

For once she had no particular fears that Boy and Angela might either disgrace themselves or her. Boy, somewhat to his own displeasure, was the innkeeper. Angela, as she had predicted from the beginning, was a singularly sanctimonious Angel of the Lord. Neither of them suffered noticeably from stage fright.

Lucy took them straight to the Manor as she had been instructed. There was no sign of Robert, but Simone was serving an enormous repast for the numerous helpers already arrived. There was a suppressed hum in the house.

A cold buffet supper was already laid out in the dining-room. One end had been turned into a bar and an impressive assortment of crates and boxes were stacked at strategic points. On one table at the far end stood an urn for brewing the mulled wine on which Adelaide had insisted. Nicholas disapproved of it and said so, but she felt that it was necessary to the tone of the evening, so he had given in. Nicholas in fact had elected to close the restaurant that evening, leaving only the snug and the saloon bar open for regular patrons, and decanted himself and his chef together with, of course, Simone, to the Manor. Robert Challenger had seemed amused at this wholesale invasion, he told Lucy, but hardly grateful.

'The truth is,' he said, pausing in his harassed counting of glasses, 'that this whole thing has got out of hand. I don't think Adelaide has any idea how much it's going to cost. Not only will she not make any money, she'll almost certainly lose some. Do you know how many tickets she's sold?'

'Well,' said Lucy cautiously, 'I had six hundred printed and there aren't any left in the office. But I don't know whether she's actually sold them for money. You know what she's like.'

'I do indeed. Free tickets for anyone who lends her a screwdriver.'

'Something like that,' admitted Lucy.

'She's a darling,' he said despairingly, 'but she's absolutely and utterly mad.'

The object of his remark descended the staircase into the passageway as he was speaking and came into the dining room, followed by Robert Challenger, who looked at Lucy quizzically.

'Oh, you've found her out at last, have you, Browning?'

118

he observed. 'Quite mad, I agree.'

'Not me,' said Lucy, blushing as if at a compliment.

Nicholas grinned. 'No. My beloved but improvident aunt. I'd be prepared to hazard money on the chance that you're in the red, Adelaide.'

'Over this?' she replied, not in the least put out. 'Well, it has been a little more costly than I anticipated. But we should make a profit of five or six hundred, I think. And Mr. Challenger has very kindly said that he'll make up anything we get to a thousand pounds which was the target the Committee decided on.'

Lucy started. 'What?'

'That seems a high price to pay for having your house turned upside down, I must say,' said Nicholas.

A shade of annoyance crossed Robert's face. 'Oh, nonsense. It's a—er—unique experience. I'm looking forward to it. What time do you think the performances can actually start?'

'Or rather more to the point, what time will they end?' demanded the irrepressible Nicholas.

His aunt quelled him. 'You don't have to stay and watch,' she said. 'You can go and eat and drink if you like. It's going to be quite informal. I want it to be a sort of drawing room entertainment. You'll find I've set the chairs in little groups rather than lining them up like a church hall. The object of the exercise, after all, is to enjoy oneself.'

'All right,' he chuckled. 'What time do we start to enjoy ourselves?'

Robert Challenger interposed, 'As I understand it, the hall will be cleared for dancing by about half-past nine. At least that's what the young men providing the music seem to think.'

'Good,' said Nicholas. 'I'll remember that.' He looked at his watch. 'It's gone six. I'd better go and change.' He sped away under Adelaide's frosty eye.

'And so had you, hadn't you, Lucy?' she remarked. 'Did you bring your dress with you, or have you got it at the cottage?'

'It's here,' said Lucy. 'But I'm to help with the school

play. I don't think I'd better change until that's finished.'

'Then you won't be able to sell programmes,' Adelaide pointed out. 'You can't stand at the doorway in gumboots and a donkey jacket. You have to look pretty and —oh, you know—in the part to sell programmes.'

'I'm sure Simone will be delighted to help,' said Robert soothingly. 'She's been dying for an excuse to array herself in her finery ever since she arrived.'

Adelaide sniffed. 'I'm sure she has.'

Much to Lucy's relief she allowed herself to be sidetracked and Robert led her off to the kitchen to persuade Simone. Lucy fled to the larger bedroom where the children were romping with gold-painted wings and false beards. Narrowly avoiding a shrewdly swung shepherd's crook, Lucy set about restoring order. There was the usual complement of little girls whose hair had been pulled and little boys who had lost their handkerchiefs. There was also a shoeless shepherd who had left his sandals at home and could not be convinced that his stout lace-ups would not show if he stood behind everyone else.

'But I don't *want* to stand at the back,' he wailed, as Lucy tried to console him.

Eventually it was agreed that he should go barefoot. This Spartan example fortunately inspired a disciple. Henry Eliot who was prone to bronchitis had been instructed by his mother that he was not to take off his scarf in this nasty damp weather. Interpreting the maternal directives literally, Henry had wound the scarf about his small person before donning his costume. Having a good clear speaking voice, he had been cast as Melchior, whose costume was scarlet. As a result he resembled nothing so much as a stout robin, and nothing more unkingly than Henry trotting perspiring in the wake of the other two kings could be imagined. But if Jack would walk barefooted on the treacherous flagstones of the hall Henry, not to be outdone, would discard his scarf. Lucy devoutly hoped that his mother would not find it out.

By half past seven, when the hum from downstairs was distinctly less subdued and a comfortable amount of laughter and clinking of glasses filtered upstairs, the play was ready. Lucy and Jane Frobisher ushered the children into the hall and Lucy retired to a seat strategically near an exit.

Someone turned out all the lights but the centre chandelier and the Christmas tree decorations and the play began. There was a slight stirring of the air round her and a figure dropped down by her chair.

'Good evening,' said Robert Challenger over his shoulder. He settled his back comfortably against the curved leg of her chair and said out of the corner of his mouth, 'I assume our charges are in this.'

Lucy looked round to see if anyone had heard. But they were all concentrating on the centre of the hall. 'They are not,' she hissed, '*ours*.'

'Of course they are.'

'That's something we'll have to discuss. There are other things too. This business of you paying for Boy's school . . .'

'Not now, there's a good girl. Come and talk to me any time you like. You're perfectly welcome.'

'Well, I will,' she said with bravado.

'Fine. But not here and now. I want to enjoy this.'

And to all appearances he began to concentrate on the play. It went no worse than it had done at rehearsal and a good deal better than might have been expected. No major disasters occurred. Mary did not drop the baby and Joseph failed to sit on the crib, both of which had enlivened earlier occasions. The innkeeper rolled his eyes horribly and the Angel of the Lord's wings managed to remain in a horizontal position. All, thought Lucy complacently, beginning to move as the last five minutes of the play started, had gone off remarkably well.

She had reckoned without Boy's ingenuity. He had a passion for realism on the stage. Jane Frobisher had, unhappily as it turned out, allowed the innkeeper a change of heart at the last moment. After the kings had presented their gifts, the shepherds made a moving little speech about owning nothing but consecrating what they had to the Child. Boy should have come in, complaining about the noise, seen the child and fallen down and worshipped with the others. To Boy, however, this simple series of events seemed both unlikely and undramatic, and with Billy Marshall's help he had effectively re-written the last scene.

The automaton chorus was just proclaiming, 'Accept our crooks, accept our sheep, accept our hearts and go to sleep,' when some lifelike baaing made itself heard.

The audience was impressed.

The fine hairs on Lucy's neck stood up in horror. 'No!' she muttered, half to herself. 'No, I don't believe it!' And then as an unmistakable clippety-clop emerged, she half rose from her seat. 'Oh no, *please* . . .'

Robert Challenger turned his head, laughed softly, seized her hand and forced her back on to the chair with one easy movement. 'You know, you have the makings of a first-class spoilsport,' he murmured. 'Shut up and watch the play.'

She could do no other. Her fascinated gaze was riveted to the little group.

'Who's left this damned sheep in my snug?' roared Boy, offstage.

There was a slight stir among the audience. This was the first time that the acting had come to life, or indeed the dialogue either. Jane Frobisher's idea of what was proper to nativity plays consisted of unlikely sentiments expressed in rigid doggerel. For the first time the audience's interest was fairly caught. If it hadn't been so appalling, thought Lucy, she would have been rather proud of Boy.

He came marching in, Billy Marshall's Daft Willy at his heels, a bottle of Nicholas's Courvoisier under his arm. Willy, an amiable but determined creature, made his way through the ranks to Billy's side, scattering shepherds heedlessly. They broke ranks and crowded round him. Boy, finding himself upstaged by the animal, cleared a space with a few wide sweeps of the arm, went down on one knee by the cradle and launched into

Miss Frobisher's verse. Billy did his best with his demoralised troops and after much hushing and shushing, had them all down on their knees as well.

Boy went back to the beginning.

Daft Willy, puzzled but not afraid, trotted among them, occasionally overturning one of the smaller and more rotund shepherds on the outskirts. Robert Challenger's shoulders began to heave.

At last, however, Daft Willy came to Boy. He could not go forward, if he went back he trod on a shepherd, and if he went sideways he tangled either with a voluminous angel or a crib. Boy stood up to make his final line the more dramatic and Willy saw escape. With a screech of fear mingled with triumph he dived between Boy's legs. Boy, caught unawares, was lifted clean off the ground and for a halcyon moment was born off on Willy's retreating rump. Then, struggling to right himself, he fell forward, ruining Miss Frobisher's touching lines, smashing the bottle he held against the crib, and deluging the Virgin Mary in Nicholas's best brandy.

'And God bless all who sail in her,' spluttered Robert Challenger, very nearly helpless with laughter.

Lucy glared at him, but the audience were delighted. They stamped and cheered and applauded and called for Boy and Daft Willy who was, in spite of Miss Frobisher's incoherent protests, led on to take his bow by a blushing Billy Marshall. There was even a charitable call of 'Author', though that was more polite than anything else and Jane Frobisher did not feel equal to responding to it.

The lights went up and the children began to straggle upstairs again. Lucy tried to wriggle away from Robert Challenger's restraining hand.

'I must go,' she said.

'No, you mustn't.'

'Yes, I must—I promised. I've got to help Jane clear things up.'

He relaxed her hand and looked up at her again, his eyes oddly bright. 'Oh, if that's all. You will come back? No sneaking off home with the children?'

'I promise,' she smiled down at him. 'Though how I shall dare hold up my head I can't think. You do realise that it's all Boy's fault? Even the sheep was his idea.'

'That was disastrously clear,' he acknowledged, bubbling over. 'He's a remarkable child. I must get to know him better. I suspect he's very like his aunt. Oh, run away and play nursemaid, if you must, but I warn you, if you try to run out on us, I'll come to the cottage and collect you.'

She touched his shoulder reassuringly. 'Don't worry. United we fall. And I'm very much afraid that we're going to fall a lot further tonight.'

'*Are* we? Good heavens! What other treats are there in store?'

She consulted the programme. 'Well, it's the madrigals next, and then the dramatic society, then me and then the dramatic society again.'

'I wouldn't miss a minute of it,' he vowed mischievously. 'Go and tend the infantry and then come back and have a drink before you perform. You'll probably need it.'

Lucy agreed privately but felt that she would be lucky if she were dressed in time. So she smiled noncommitally and left him.

Upstairs all was chaos as the dramatic society members tried to disentangle their wigs and buckled shoes from the flying beards and crooks. Tempers ran high and Lucy was fully occupied. In the distance she was aware of Jane Frobisher's vengeful regard and was glad to be busy. Boy, of course, was deplorably unrepentant. With your true actor's instinct for audience response he felt he had done well and was bursting with pride. Told by Lucy that he would only be allowed to come downstairs and listen to the rest of the entertainment if he promised to be a *good* boy, he gave her a beguiling grin and said he would just as soon go home. She found it irresistible and hugged him.

'Well, at least be quiet,' she begged him. 'And keep out of Miss Frobisher's way.'

He nodded. Lucy's last warning was really unnecessary, his look said. When she released him he scampered away like a hare and disappeared in the direction of the kitchen with his cronies, Angela in attendance. Finding that the dramatic society members were sitting tensely on the stairs awaiting their turn, Lucy went to change.

The room looked as if a small hurricane had whipped through, but it was at least quiet. It looked even a little sad, an odd plimsoll discarded in the middle of the floor and a rejected shawl lying on top of a pile of untidy costumes. The dressing table, which had been used by the ladies as a make-up table, was covered with sticks of matte greasepaint, sinister little pots of rouge and eye-shadow so dark it looked almost black. Lucy picked it up and sniffed it. There was a thick, sweet smell to it that she found oddly unpleasant. It reminded her of something which she could not identify. She put it down and began, a little wearily, to change into her own costume.

Adelaide had been right—the dress flattered her. In the end she had made it up in a furnishing fabric she had found, which was printed in alternate soft pink and silver-grey stripes. It had a sheen to it, so that the stripes were almost undistinguishable, and the dress merely looked as if it were a rich pink that had been dusted over with some powder that had taken the harshness from the shade. The deep ivory lace that Adelaide had presented her with added to this cobwebby effect. Adelaide had been most impressed when Lucy showed it to her.

'You really do look a period piece,' she had said thoughtfully. 'Sort of muted. *Very* graceful.' And she had spoilt it all by adding, '*That* ought to show Nicholas!'

It had almost destroyed Lucy's pleasure in the dress. She had immediately changed the subject, but the remark came back to her now as she shook out her stiff skirts, and smoothed one well-cut sleeve. Oh well, there was nothing so terrible in it after all. She would put on her locket, take her lute and go and play, and then she could take the children home. She need not see Nicholas at all. For a moment she was surprised to find herself hoping to avoid him. 'Perhaps I'm recovering,' she thought wryly, tying the velvet ribbon from which her locket was suspended behind her neck.

Picking up the little pot of eye-shadow, she sniffed it, suddenly remembering where she had found that perfume before. It was Simone's. She looked at the littered dressing table. Of course, all this must belong to Simone, who had generously put it at the disposal of Adelaide Browning's companions. Lucy ran a finger round the surface of the stuff. It was dark as midnight and greasy. She applied it audaciously to an eyelid and found that it was a good deal less offensive in colour than she had expected. In fact it was a rather charming china blue. She settled down enjoyably to paint her face with Simone's cosmetics and spent so long over it that only the sound of applause for the dramatic society's offering recalled her to a sense of her surroundings. Seizing her lute out of its canvas case, she fled down the stairs. There was no time for stage fright.

She had prepared three pieces, all of them early seventeenth century. They were short, melodic, and clearly pleased her audience enormously. To finish she played a little jig which set them tapping their toes. She finished with an abrupt, mischievous rippling chord. Standing up, she bowed her head in acknowledgement and while the clapping was still rising to a crescendo, slipped out of the Hall.

Robert was waiting for her.

'I thought you tried to run away,' he said in satisfied tones, stopping her with his hands on either side of her arms. He held her away from him. 'Why have you run away?'

'I've exhausted my repertoire,' said Lucy primly and untruthfully. 'I daren't risk being pressed for an encore.'

He laughed. 'All right, I'll accept that. Come and talk to me.'

'Talk?' She was flustered, suspicious.

'*You* said you wanted to talk to me,' he reminded her blandly. 'If you don't want to be swamped with admiration and congratulations, come into a quiet corner with

me and talk. I'll draw you some of that spiced wine—
You must need it. You didn't come down again after
you went upstairs with the children, did you?'

'No,' she admitted.

'So you let those brats pull you to pieces for the second
time this evening. And I'll bet you haven't had a decent
meal all day. I'll get some salad for you before the horde
descends on the dining-room.'

'You're very kind,' said Lucy, startled.

'And you're very complimentary for once. It makes a
nice change. Keep it up.' He patted her cheek. 'Go and
put your instrument in cotton wool and join me in the
library.'

Lucy stared at him, her eyes enormous. Then,
wordlessly, she obeyed him, running upstairs, her skirts
bunched in trembling hands, the lute an ungainly
weight in her arms.

When she reached the dressing-room she found that
tears had coursed their way down her cold cheeks all
unnoticed. She blotted them with a careful finger. It
was foolish to cry tonight. For once he was being quite
kind to her. He was almost approachable. At any rate
she did not feel afraid of him. This tearful melancholy
was as unjustified as it was unappealing.

She joined him some fifteen minutes later, having
carefully blotted those same tears and added yet another
film of Simone's face powder to an already substantial
coating. Some devil of defiance had prompted her to
shade her eyes so that they glowed a little more brightly,
to colour her mouth a little more vividly. Escaping from
the oppressively scented bedroom, she caught a glimpse
of herself in one of the long mirrors. The lace at her
elbows was still stirring with the movement. Otherwise,
she thought, startled, she might be one of Adelaide's
exquisite porcelain cocottes, as sweetly sophisticated as
Simone herself. At the thought tears rose again and she
dashed them away with the back of her hand, closing
the door with a snap behind her.

She knocked timidly on the library door and had to
knock again before Robert heard her. It was in darkness

except for the rosy glow cast by the fire. Someone must have been in here this evening to make it up, because it was burning merrily. Robert himself was in shadow, standing by the desk out of the warm cone of light cast by the fire. To her amazement Lucy saw that he had indeed filled a tray with food. Her eyes widened. She could see his silhouette, a glass of some dark vermilion wine in his hand. His face was in shadow.

He looked at her for a moment as she stood in the doorway, her laces and ribbons fluttering from her speed.

Then—'Ah yes,' he said, almost as if he had forgotten, which in view of that loaded tray was ridiculous. 'Lucy. Come in. You must be starving.'

'Hence the midnight feast?' she asked, relieved by his bantering tone. She had expected—she did not know what—something different. Just now when she had come into this room and seen him so dark and suddenly remote, she had felt a return of her old panic. Taking herself to task, she closed the door with fingers that shook slightly. Then she went to the desk and surveyed the groaning tray. 'I don't think I'm *that* hungry.'

He shrugged. 'Leave it for the moment, then. But have some wine. It's been polluted with cloves and other garbage, I'm afraid, but at least it's warm.'

'You think I need warming up as well?' she said lightly.

'I do indeed.' There was amusement in his voice. 'Come and sit by the fire. Tell me what you wanted to say.'

She followed him obediently and sank down on the rug. 'I don't think I can,' she said frankly. 'Not just like that. I have long arguments with you in my head, but they never seem to come out like that when I'm talking to you.'

'They wouldn't,' he drawled.

'Why?'

'Because I don't say the same things when you're talking to me as I do when I'm in your head.'

She thought about it. 'Yes, I suppose that's the
128

trouble. I can refute all the arguments I've thought of. Only some I haven't.'

'Well, that's honest. Though I don't recall us arguing.'

'That's only because I'm too afraid of you,' she confessed, brave in the firelight.

'*What?*' He was honestly astounded.

'Well, of what you might do, then,' she amended. 'To the children.'

'My dear girl, I may live in Dracula's Castle, but I haven't yet come to the stage of carrying off children,' he said with irony.

'No, I meant *my* children.' She stopped. 'Peter's children,' she corrected herself. 'I thought you'd make me give them up.'

'My dear child, why on earth should I?' He looked down at her. 'Do you want to get rid of them and be off to pastures new like Peter?'

She looked up quickly. 'Oh no. *No*, of course not. I'd be only too happy if they could stay with me for ever.'

'Ah,' he said, stroking his chin. 'Now there's a difficulty.'

'You mean you're determined to send Boy away to school,' she said, her voice breaking for all her brave pretence at self-possession.

'Well, I don't think he'll be welcome back at Miss Frobisher's establishment after tonight's jamboree, do you?' he asked.

'Oh, don't laugh about it! Jane Frobisher would get over it.'

'Yes, but would Boy? He's much too lively to be confined with children younger than himself and by far less intelligent. He'll be up to all sorts of mischief. And where he leads the little girl will follow, as I've already seen.'

'Angela will be all right. I'm giving her a puppy for Christmas.'

'Are you indeed?' His voice was silky, but it had taken on that dangerous note Lucy had come to recognise. 'I suppose it didn't occur to you to ask my opinion?'

'It occurred to me,' she said steadily, 'but I decided

it was none of your business. You're not a member of the family, after all. As far as I'm concerned you're just acting as a sort of bailiff for Peter until he comes back.'

'How dare you speak to me like that?' he snapped, suddenly furious.

'You're nothing to do with the family,' she insisted on a high, unstable note. 'I won't have you for family. All I want is to be left alone with the children. All this dictating, and sending Boy away and paying for it with your own damned money. And forbidding the children to do things. It's none of your business!'

With a gasp, she broke off at a savage movement of his. She sprang up, but he pursued her. For an instant she thought he would hit her and then, fearfully, realised his intention was very different.

'No!' She would have fled from him then, but he held her with both hands.

In the shadows as they were she could not make out his expression or even his features. Crazily he was a stranger, breathing unevenly in the dark like a disturbed prowler. He had her hard against him. The stuff of his coat scratched her cold flesh. Eyes dilating, she stared up at him, straining to find something familiar or reassuring in the bending shadow.

He found the soft painted mouth without any gentleness. Lucy was shivering again, but this time the cold came from the inmost marrow of her bones. She closed her eyes in a kind of despair. What was she doing here in the dark with a man who did not want her, who wanted —if he wanted anyone at all, for more than a passing moment, which she rather doubted—the beautiful sophisticate he disparagingly referred to as Nicholas Browning's bit of fluff.

Locking cold fingers behind his neck, she gave him kiss for kiss, defiantly.

Robert lifted his head. Lucy thought she heard him laugh very softly, then with a fingertip he began to caress her face as if he were drawing a cobweb over it. There was, she acknowledged sadly, a deadly expertise to it. Her fingers tightened and obediently he lowered his head, but this time his lips found, not her devastated mouth, but the corner of her eyelids, her ears, her throat. Almost casually he untied the black velvet thread and the silver locket slipped, warm, down her flesh. He kissed the hollow where her pulse fluttered.

Her breath caught, half in wonder, half in protest. He heard it and looked up, holding her away from him as if he could see her clearly.

'This should have happened weeks ago,' he pronounced.

Lucy's hands went to her cheeks. 'But it doesn't *settle* anything,' she said miserably.

'There are better ways of resolving differences than by the inordinate amount of verbiage in which you take so much delight,' he told her sententiously. 'It's all quite simple. The children need security and a stable background.'

'And love,' interjected Lucy swiftly.

He sighed. 'All right—and love. Which you give them. But they do need stability. As I've already had occasion to point out, you're quite mad, therefore they need someone else for the stability ingredient. I'm positively immovable. Marry me, and then they'll have everything they need.'

'How *dare* you?' she gasped. It sounded like the grossest insult, yet in that light caressing voice she could not be sure whether Robert was teasing her or not. She could not make out his intention and felt oddly foolish, still in his arms, trying to make up her mind whether she ought to be offended.

'Oh, I dare, I dare, my sweet silly Lucy. I dare a great deal . . .'

And then he dragged her ruthlessly back against him, hands urgent with dainty dress and ordered curls.

Then improbably, impossibly, the door opened and Adelaide Browning appeared at it.

'Robert,' she was saying agitatedly, 'the Wild children are making a terrible noise. Lucy seems to have disappeared and Angela's having hysterics . . .' Then she broke off. Her eyes accustoming themselves to the dark,

131

she made out a dishevelled girl in her host's arms, and he, clearly, passionately absorbed in her. 'Forgive me,' she said, distressed. Robert hardly glanced at her. 'I'll go and look upstairs. She must be somewhere. I'm so sorry— Robert—' She was closing the door, but added one fatal, final broadside—'Simone.'

Lucy stiffened. Feeling it, he kissed her swiftly, harshly. She whipped out of his arms and fled behind the armchair. Her knees were trembling. Robert made no protest or attempt to follow her, merely stood quietly where she had left him, watching her. It occurred to her that the firelight must be playing full on her face, and her hands flew to her cheeks.

'Oh, my God,' she muttered, loathing herself. 'Oh *no*!'

Still silent, he observed her distress. Indignation rose in her. She might be a fool, but it was not chivalrous of him to make it so obvious. She swallowed.

'We'd better go back,' she said.

'Lucy . . .'

But she interrupted. 'No, please.' A wry smile. 'I think we've finished everything we have to say to each other.'

'I haven't finished,' he said with such bland assurance that, briefly, her temper flickered again.

'But I have,' she said firmly. Insultingly she added, 'Just how much do you think your money entitles you to, Robert?'

The shadow figure went rigid. 'Rather less than you, apparently. I hadn't realised that filthy lucre figured so largely in your life. But you can dismiss it from your mind. There's no debt. Whatever I may do for the children has nothing to do with you.' His voice became biting. 'You don't have to try to repay me in your own peculiar coinage.'

Where had it gone, that shared laughter, that better understanding on which she had congratulated herself earlier?

Lucy drew a shaky breath and controlled the cascade of tears that threatened. She found she wanted to rage

132

and scream as well as weep. She wanted above all to insult him as deeply and hurtfully as he had insulted her.

'I'm glad to hear it,' she snapped, and marched out of the room.

CHAPTER VIII

The children when she found them were in the kitchen being made much of by Nicholas. Angela was in tears, but to Lucy's harassed eye that looked more the result of over-excitement than any great fears of having been abandoned by her aunt. In fact both Boy and Angela were bright-eyed from lack of sleep and bouncing with a hysterical energy that did not augur well for either a peaceful night or the next day. Glancing at the kitchen clock, Lucy found to her amazement that it was already past ten o'clock.

'Time to go home,' she said firmly. 'I'm exhausted, even if you aren't. And if you aren't,' she added meanly to Boy, 'you should be.'

He looked smug. 'I can stay awake all night,' he boasted.

'I devoutly hope you won't, however.' She took the handkerchief from Nicholas's hand and gave Angela's face a brisk final wipe. 'It's all right, Nicholas, I really do want to go home. And Boy and Angela aren't upset or anything. They're just over-excited. They've probably over-eaten too,' she added gloomily.

Nicholas said concernedly, 'Are you all right? You've been off colour for days, according to Adelaide. And you do look peaky now.'

Lucy gave a little laugh which broke. '*Not* a flatterer, are you, Nicholas? Really, I'm fine. I'm just tired.' How tired, she thought, weariness dragging the flesh off her bones nearly. 'I wish I hadn't got to drive back,' she said involuntarily.

Nicholas looked worried. 'If you can wait, I'll take you. I must stay and serve supper. But after that . . .'

She shook herself. 'Oh, nonsense. It's very kind of you, but it's too silly. You'd either take the Land Rover and leave it at the cottage and have to walk back, or else take your car and then I'd have to come back for the big one. It's not practical. I'm just being lazy.'

'But I don't think you ought to drive. You look all in.' He thought. '*I* know—Simone can run you back in my car. Then I'll bring the Land Rover back later and I'll walk home. I don't want to stay here too late anyway. It'll be a good excuse to get away. I'll tell Simone.'

Lucy flushed. 'Perhaps she won't want to turn out,' she murmured hopefully. 'It's a dreadful imposition. You can't ask her to, Nicholas.'

'I can tell her to,' he said arrogantly. 'I'm her employer, though she seems to forget it when it doesn't suit her convenience.'

Lucy was taken aback. 'You're hardly her employer when it comes to driving people around. She's a waitress, not a chauffeur,' she protested.

'She'll do what I tell her,' he returned loudly. 'Get your lute and put the children's coats on. If there's anything you want brought back to the cottage put it in the Land Rover or leave me a list.'

He went in search of Simone. Quite cowed, Lucy began to button Angela into her velvet coat and bonnet, losing one of her woollen mittens under the Welsh dresser in the process. Boy retrieved it, emerging triumphantly covered with dust just as Simone walked into the kitchen. She looked perfectly pleasant, smiled at Boy and said to Lucy, 'Nicholas tells me you're tired. I'm not surprised.'

Something in her expression rather than her tone, which was warm with sympathy, made Lucy wary. It was almost as if the girl said that weariness was to be expected in one of her advanced years.

I feel old enough tonight in all conscience, thought Lucy dispiritedly. A hundred years at least.

'Are you ready to go? I'll run you back with pleasure, but I mustn't be long.' Simone made it sound as if her presence was indispensable to the festivities. And perhaps it was, Lucy acknowledged.

'You're very good,' she said. 'If you'd put the children

in the car, I'll just run upstairs and get my lute.'

She was afraid she might meet Robert in this last desperate effort of hers in his house, but by good fortune she did not. She went out into the bitter night, promising herself that she would not return to the Manor ever. It was not a melodramatic promise, rather a comforting one. She felt as if she had been stripped of every defence by an enemy immeasurably better armed than herself without ever quite discovering the grounds on which they were fighting. But however confused she might be about the cause, there was no doubt in her mind as to who had one. She accomplished the journey to Hazel Cottage in painful silence.

When they arrived, Simone helped the children out and they ran at once to the back door which was always left unlocked.

'Thank you,' said Lucy, recalled to a sense of her surroundings. She gathered her lute to her and made to get out of the car, but Simone stopped her.

'No, wait a moment. I'm glad to have this opportunity of talking to you. I mustn't stay, but I'd like— well, it's difficult—I don't quite know how to put it.'

'Put what?' asked Lucy, bewildered. 'Look, Simone, I'm tired. I'm very tired. To be honest, I'm just a bit ratty. So far I've kept my temper with Boy and Angela, but it's wearing thin. I would hate to lose it with you when you've been kind enough to bring us home.'

'I don't want to make you angry.' Simone sounded hurt. 'I only wanted to —well—*hint . . .*'

Lucy closed her eyes. 'I'm far beyond taking hints. If there's something you want to say, say it, for God's sake, and get it over with.'

'It's just that—I'm going up to London after Christmas.'

'Oh,' said Lucy, blankly. 'Congratulations. I'm very glad for you if that's what you want. But couldn't the glad tidings have waited until I'm awake?'

Simone ignored that. 'With Robert,' she blurted, and sank back in her seat as if she had burnt her boats and waited to see what Lucy would do about it.

'Robert?' said Lucy slowly. She found she was incredulous. 'You do mean Robert Challenger?'

Simone nodded.

Lucy felt as if the pit of her stomach had simply fallen away, quite suddenly, leaving only very cold space. 'Congratulations,' she said again, emptily.

Simone seemed disappointed. 'It's not—that is, we're not telling anyone in the village. I shall just leave.'

'A good idea,' said the zombie by her side.

'Of course, I shan't come back. We've decided that already. I shall carry on with my career in London and that's where we'll be together.'

Lucy drew back, a little disgusted by the undisguised complacency of her tone.

'That will be nice. I don't see why I'm particularly favoured with this confidence, though. Do you want me to send your mail on or something? Wouldn't Nicholas be a more appropriate confidant in that case?'

Simone laid a soft hand on her arm. It was a pretty gesture and one which Lucy had seen her use before. She drew her arm away.

'That's just it—I—I can't tell him. He'll be so hurt. I thought—perhaps—you might tell him. Once I've gone, you know, and he's got over this crush he's got on me.'

Lucy was outraged. She felt the fury wash through her in a reviving tide and opened the car door.

'I shall do no such thing,' she said precisely. 'It's no concern of mine. And I shouldn't worry yourself to death about Nicholas's broken heart. No doubt he'll survive the blow.'

She marched vaingloriously indoors while the wind whipped her eighteenth-century skirts about her ankles and blew her hair across her mouth. Once indoors she found she was shaking with temper and a storm of tears that she had been suppressing too long. The children were singing happily, running from one bedroom to the other to recount all the glories of the night's doings. She laid her head on her two hands on the kitchen table, and enjoyed a bout of weeping the like of which she had not known since she was sixteen.

The children had subsided finally by the time Lucy raised her head. She was very stiff and cold and almost dazed with tiredness. The walk upstairs to bed seemed impossible. She brushed some cold water over her eyelids to revive her, then took a long drink of water.

Outside in the lane a car drew up. It must be Nicholas returning the Land Rover. Lucy hoped he would not want to come into the cottage. All he needed to do was put the keys through the letter box. She clenched her hands, willing him with all her might to leave the keys and go. But even as she did so, she heard his step on the path.

He scratched on the door. 'May I come in?' he called softly.

Lucy opened it perforce. 'Ssh!' she said in a less than welcoming tone.

'Children asleep?'

'I hope so. They were much too excited. I only hope they're not ill tomorrow.'

'They're tougher than that,' he said lightly. 'If you ask me young Boy will be pleased as punch with himself tomorrow. Probably be offering autographs to his admirers.'

'Don't even suggest such a thing,' Lucy begged. '*Particularly* not in his hearing. He'd no doubt think it was a good idea.'

'He's a devilish child,' Nicholas said admiringly. 'I don't give much for his chances when Jane Frobisher goes on the warpath, though. Do you?'

'It's only for a few more days. He's going to the Cathedral School in January.'

Nicholas raised his eyebrows. 'Is he indeed? That's a very sudden decision. Why did you make it?'

'I didn't. And it's not sudden. It's Peter's notion.'

'Oh yes, I remember you were worried about Peter's intentions earlier in the year. I must say this is a very sensible idea. With only one of them left at home you might find a little time for your own affairs. I suppose there's no chance of Angela going to?'

He sounded so hopeful that Lucy had a hysterical desire to laugh. 'Not to a boys' school,' she replied.

'And you don't want her to go anyway,' he submitted. He put an affectionate arm round her shoulders. 'You're a sentimental idiot, Lucy.'

She dropped her head against his shoulder. 'I dare say I am. I can't help it. Don't bully me, Nicholas. I've had too much to bear today and I just might burst into tears.'

Nicholas was concerned. Lifting her chin, he studied her face thoughtfully. 'It looks to me as if you already have. What's wrong?'

Lucy sniffed. 'Everything,' she said comprehensively. 'I'm sorry, I'm frightful company at the moment. You'd better leave me. Are those the keys?'

He handed them to her. 'I don't like leaving you like this. You're not normally melancholic.'

She shrugged. 'I'm tired. I'll be better after a night's sleep.'

'You need a holiday,' he said abruptly. 'You've been working too hard too long. Why didn't anyone notice?'

'Nonsense,' she said. 'This is just—oh, temporary. It's been rather a hectic autumn, one way and another.'

'It certainly has.' He sat down at the kitchen table and began to play with the oven glove that she had left on it. 'With the Manor, and Challenger and Simone, and all.' He looked up at her quickly. 'Did you know Simone is leaving?'

'She was bound to eventually,' she replied evasively. 'She's hardly going to be a village waitress all her life.'

'No.' He folded the glove in four and then released it, watching it absorbedly as it sprang back to its original shape. 'I thought she might be—persuaded to stay. But I was wrong.'

'I'm sorry.' It was almost automatic.

'Are you? I'm not—Not now. It would have been a big mistake. She's not a kind girl.'

'I didn't know you were looking for kindness,' she observed dryly.

'Nor did I.' He laughed, a comically ingenuous expression crossing his face. 'But I thought this evening—when she was making up, actually. She wouldn't give anyone else any room at the glass until she'd finished—she's really very selfish. She may look like a child, but she would be most uncomfortable to live with.'

Lucy heard this remarkable confidence with some surprise. He saw it and, leaning over, took her hands in both his.

'I'm making a pretty bad fist of it, aren't I? The trouble is I've never done anything like this before.'

'Like what?' Lucy was quite bewildered.

'Like asking an old friend to marry me,' he said calmly.

She stared at him. He laughed.

'You're not very complimentary, Lucy my love, Don't look so stunned.'

'B-but I am,' she managed.

He stood up and came to her, holding her comfortably in his arms.

'Think about it,' he urged. 'We have a lot in common. We've known each other a long time. I know you're soft in the head about those children. And you know I'm a susceptible clown.'

'Ah yes.' Lucy gently disengaged herself. 'And that's what this is all about, isn't it? The perfidious Simone. Nicholas, my dear, you are what is commonly known as on the rebound. You'd better go home and sleep it off.'

'Rubbish.' He took her back in his arms. '*Listen* to me, Lucy. I've been a fool over Simone, I admit it. But it wasn't such a bad thing. She looked so pretty and sort of helpless, and I wanted to take care of her.'

'So?'

'So when I saw you tonight, I realised you weren't any different really.' He gave an ashamed laugh. 'It's stupid —I always think of you as a capable child. I suppose it's because you never tagged round after Peter and me when we were children. You always seemed to have something of your own to do, to be quite self-sufficient.'

'Thank you!'

'Only I don't believe that any more. When I saw you this evening—you looked so pale—and Adelaide was right about that dress, it makes you look completely different. Sort of distant and unattainable as if you were at the wrong end of a telescope.'

Lucy sighed. 'Nicholas, are you seriously telling me that this extraordinary proposal of yours is the result of my appearing in fancy dress?'

He looked annoyed. 'I was trying to *explain*.'

'You don't need to explain anything. I understand perfectly well.'

'You don't believe me.'

'Yes, I do. I believe you implicitly. You want a wife who looks like Columbine and behaves like Cinderella. It's very charming of you. But I am not a candidate. I'm not like that, as you know very well.'

I must be mad, she thought. This is all I've ever wanted, ever since I left school, being offered to me. She ran her hands over her eyes in an ineffably weary gesture.

'Please go, Nicholas. I'm sorry, but I can't marry you. It's quite impossible. And in the light of day you'll see it just as clearly as I do now.'

'But—'

'*Please* don't keep on about it,' she cried, her control slipping dangerously. 'Good night.'

He went without a word.

Lucy drooped against the wall, laying her hot cheek against the window to cool it. Forlornly she thought, he'll never come back after that, and was surprised to find the prospect a relief. She examined her feelings. It was as if she had become so used to her devotion to Nicholas that she had not really noticed it was waning. But it had disappeared altogether. She liked him, he was a familiar and generous friend. But he roused her to impatient fury with his hesitations and his flights of fancy. And her practical approach to life, she realised, would become equally annoying to him. Wasn't Adelaide always telling her that she was too unromantic?

Well, it was true. Nicholas more than anyone, she knew, would want his wife to be a romantic creature.

It was a lowering discovery. She was no longer in love with Nicholas. She probably was not capable of being in love with anyone. She had turned into a fussy old hen with not a thought in her head beyond the children's welfare. The only time she forgot to be circumspect and civil was when she was quarrelling with Robert about the children.

She stood up abruptly as if she had burnt herself.

'No,' she said out loud to the awful idea that had come to her. It was not possible that, of all the safe respectable men she knew, every one of them as stuffy as herself, she should have fallen in love with the single maverick among them. Thinking of his wicked smile—'No,' she said again more uncertainly.

It was outrageous. It was stupid. If she was unsuited to Nicholas, Robert Challenger was way out of her league. At least she had the sense to recognise that. On the other hand, when he was not insulting her and terrorising her, he did make her laugh.

She must put such an idea out of her mind. It would destroy all her peace. He would be gone soon, if Simone were to be believed. She must simply avoid him until he left. No doubt she would recover from him as soon as she had from Nicholas. But it was bravado and she knew it. She would not recover quickly at all. She had nursed her affection for Nicholas, she had half wanted to be in love with him. This new sensation had sprung itself on her uninvited and unwelcome. Not knowing how she came by it, she was at a loss to guess how she would rid herself of it. She did know, though she was palpably reluctant to admit it, that it would take a very long time indeed.

The last few days of term were embarrassing. Jane Frobisher treated Boy with disdain and Lucy with compassion. The situation was not helped by the fact that whenever she encountered Miss Frobisher Lucy had a lunatic desire to giggle.

There was a great deal of work to be done, not least

at the Manor. Lucy organised a party of Boy Scouts under the Vicar's direction to dismantle the decorations and deliver Christmas trees to their allotted recipients. She did not visit the house herself. She assumed that Simone was making herself responsible for any more precise cleaning of the house than the strict removal of foreign bodies from the Hall. Adelaide was a frequent visitor and seemed to have come to think highly of Robert Challenger. Seeing the amount of the cheque which she paid into Mrs. Browning's Roman Way fund signed by him, Lucy was not surprised. It disappointed her to find the Brownings influenced in such a way, but in this she did them an injustice. Colonel Browning in particular had found a kindred spirit in the man. He began telling Lucy of the fellow's excellent company one day and found her so unresponsive that his bushy eyebrows flew up into his hair. It was not like Lucy to put up barriers when her employers wanted to chat. He wondered if she were ill and resolved her to give her a good long holiday over the Christmas week. He would discuss it with Adelaide.

'Best give her a holiday before Christmas so she can do her shopping,' his wife replied, when he told her of his benevolent scheme. 'And tell her to leave Boy and Angela with us. She won't want them trailing round after her when she's buying their presents.'

The Colonel retailed this to Lucy. 'Go when you like,' he said. 'Tomorrow. This afternoon if you want. Young Nicholas could give you a lift. He's going into Newbury today.'

She said hastily that tomorrow would be better. She would have to get some money and by the time Nicholas arrived in Newbury the banks would be shut.

Colonel Browning gave her a shrewd look under his brows. It was a pity, he thought, that women, even such admirable quiet creatures as Lucy, were so capricious. He said nothing except to agree to receive the children the following day.

There was a light powdering of snow on the ground when Lucy set off the next morning. There had been snow on the hill for a couple of days, but none that had fallen in the valley had lain longer than a couple of hours. In spite of the bitter wind the ground was still not yet frozen, much to Angela and Boy's disgust. They wanted to make a snowman. Last year Lucy had made one for them which was the first such creation they had ever seen, and now they were impatient to repeat the feat. They began to work with desperate speed in the yard at the Home Farm, rolling such snow there was into an insecure ball and stationing it in the middle of the yard. They were obviously happy and—until the snow melted—would be no trouble to Adelaide. Lucy adjured them to be good, a poor-spirited remark to which they paid no attention, and drove off.

When she drove back it was with a loaded car and in a much happier frame of mind. She had spent with uncharacteristic recklessness, feeling that the future was so uncertain it was as well to enjoy today. The children, used to only the most Spartan of fare, would undoubtedly be sick on all the goodies with which she intended to ply them during the Christmas season. She had even bought enough food and knick-knacks to give an impromptu children's party if the mood took her. There was a strong element of defiance mixed with her enjoyment and she knew it. Nevertheless, it was good to be cheerful again for whatever dubious motives.

She drove into the yard singing.

The children's snowman was steadily melting in his central place. There was no sign of them or the Brownings either. Lucy called out, but no one answered. Sighing, she got out of the car and went into the kitchen. It was deserted, but there was a note from Adelaide pinned on the door, clearly intended for her daily help. Apparently Mrs. Frobisher had called and Mrs. Browning had gone with her to an urgent meeting of the Roman Way Fund Committee. The money for the butcher was in the kitchen door.

Lucy frowned. There was no mention of the children. Surely she would have said if she had taken them with her. The suspicion that Adelaide had actually forgotten her small charges could not quite be banished. Perhaps she had entrusted them to her husband's sole care. Her heart in her mouth, Lucy hurried across to the office. That too was empty, except for Colonel Browning's pipe, discarded on the desk. She sighed in relief, holding on to the door sill. They must be with Colonel Browning.

But even as she was thinking it, the Land Rover bounced into the yard, Colonel Browning at the wheel and clearly unaccompanied. Lucy ran across to him.

'Where are they?'

'They? Who? What? Don't bother me now, Lucy m'dear. I've got to call the vet. One of the cows looks as if she's broken her leg, poor beast.'

'The children,' cried Lucy, almost frantic. 'Where are the children? What's happened to Boy and Angela?'

'They're about somewhere,' he returned, astonished at such an irrelevant question from a girl normally as sensible as Lucy. 'How should I know where? See Adelaide. She's in the house.'

'But she's not. She's gone out.'

'Well, they'll be with her, then.' He strode past her into the office and was already dialling the vet's number. 'Or what about the Royal Oak? They could have run off to see Nicholas.'

'They wouldn't. They know they're not allowed to cross the main road on their own.'

He looked at her over the telephone. 'Well then, perhaps they've taken the dogs out for a walk. Up the hill or somewhere . . .'

'Along the river,' she gasped. 'Boy has been stuffed with pride all week. He's still smarting from the telling off Robert gave him. And I never endorsed it because I thought he'd been frightened enough. He could have gone back there, just to show us.'

'He'll be all right as long as the dogs are with him,' said the Colonel callously. 'Sensible things, dogs.'

'But Angela!' Lucy almost screamed.

'Oh well, of course, she's not sensible,' her employer agreed.

But he spoke to empty air. She was already half way
145

down the road to the churchyard. She knew the way the children would have taken—through the Manor orchard and down to the river bank. The grass was slippery with wet snow that lay, here crisp, here a melting muddy slush, in uneven patches. Lucy wallowed through it, nearly losing her balance more than once and soaking her shoes and trousers.

As soon as she was in the orchard itself, forcing her way through goose grass and nettles, she began to call in a thin voice. There was no answer, reasonably enough, as nobody further than five yards away could possibly have heard her. Her heart in her mouth, she struck out doggedly for the river.

Almost at once she could hear children's voices and the excited yapping of dogs. At first she thought they were playing and a great wave of thankfulness rose in her throat. She stopped running, a hand pressed to her side, breathing hard.

Then she heard Boy's voice, high and filled with panic. Her first thought was that he was drowning and she flung herself headlong down the bank. Once out of the trees she could see clearly. The dogs were circling madly while Boy and Nicholas's huge dripping wolfhound stood on the stepping stones.

Lucy shot forward. 'Stand still,' she called to Boy, supposing him to be incapable of moving. 'Don't move. I'm coming!'

But he shouted back unintelligibly. The wolfhound was lolloping in and out of the water as if it were all a great game, but Boy did not seem alarmed by or even aware of his antics. He was staring, horrified at the water which gurgled past the stones. The river was swollen with melting snow and much higher than normal. It was a little affair as rivers go, but fast moving, and it swirled dangerously at the curve just past the stepping stones. Lucy, who had swum in it often, knew just how dangerous that whirlpool current could be to a small boy, although the river, even at its present height, could hardly be more than five feet deep.

Boy waved his hands at her. 'No. No!' he was shouting.

'Angela—Angela. Angela's fallen in!'

Lucy stopped dead. For a horrible moment she did not believe him. There was no sign of the little girl in the water. Lucy swallowed dryly, feeling very cold and stricken. It was as if a film in which she had no part were unrolling before her eyes. Then she found Angela, a pathetic tangle of drifting hair, carried helplessly round the bend of the bank. She threw off her coat and plunged into the eddying water.

I don't even know if she can swim, she thought academically.

She waded into the middle and tried to reach Angela, who was being swept downstream towards the stepping stones. She must have fallen in considerably higher up. She did not appear to be swimming, or even to be conscious, and from time to time water washed over her, covering her completely. While she was thus obscured from her panic-stricken aunt's view, Boy began to wail.

'She's drowned,' he screeched. 'She's drowned!'

Lucy shouted back over her shoulder, 'Nonsense,' though she was by no means sure it was. 'Go and fetch Robert.' She spared Boy a single glance. 'Quickly! Get Robert.'

He fled across the stones, sure-footed as an antelope and, with all the dogs yelping round him, sped up to the house. The noise, she thought desperately, ought to bring the fox from his lair before Boy actually got to his door.

She lost her footing and found she had to swim. The water was very swift and she made almost no progress. She tried to cut across at an angle towards Angela. The little girl was being swept closer and closer to the bank on the far side. Lucy half swam, half floundered to a point at which she judged she could cut her off and prevent her from hitting herself against the rocks from which the stepping stones had originally been constructed.

It could only have been a matter of seconds, but Lucy felt she was in that terrible race against the current for hours. Every stroke seemed unimaginably slow and

147

feeble. At last she reached Angela. Seizing the cold little face in her hands, she trod water, looking over her shoulder. The rocks advanced and she found that, supporting Angela, she was almost powerless to resist the pull of the river. Desperately she began to steer away from the bank, but it was against the stream which inexorably overcame her resistance. She was buffeted against the rocks over and over again, steadfastly keeping Angela's face above water.

At last there were cries from the bank and she looked up to see Boy waving at her as Robert Challenger made his way across the stepping stones.

'This way!' he called.

She was almost exhausted, certainly too exhausted to respond, and he saw it. Gingerly, one hand still hanging on to the edge of the stone from which he stepped, he slid into the water. He reached out a hand to her.

'Pass the child to me,' he said urgently. 'Give her to me.'

It was almost beyond her strength to obey him. After two unsuccessful attempts she succeeded in hooking the collar of Angela's bright red anorak over his outstretched fingers. He hauled the slight, unconscious body towards him. As the current caught her, the little girl's legs swung out away from the bank and he staggered. But he managed to retain his hold on the stone and brought her safe to land.

Seeing him climb up with Angela in his arms Lucy gave a great sigh of thankfulness. Her limbs were aching, her shoulders were bruised and grazed from their pounding against the stones of the bank. She was deathly cold. Wearily she made for the stepping stones. But she was too tired to hold out against the current which whirled her, almost playfully, on its own path downstream. Once again she heard Boy shouting, but in the distance. It was a not unpleasant sensation to be carried resistless by the water. She closed her eyes.

The current tossed her on to a jagged outpost of rock and a sharp pain invaded her head. Then the water closed about her ears and she heard no more.

Something warm and rough passed over her face. She moaned. It came again and she turned her head away. Somewhere a child was crying. Her face was sticky. Lucy opened her eyes.

She was lying on the bank, Rusty licking her face rhythmically. Behind him Boy was rocking backwards and forwards keening, while Robert was supporting Angela. The little girl was leaning over the river being violently sick.'

'Oh no!' murmured Lucy. This time he would be furious. And this time he would have every right to be.

He turned his head. 'You're awake, are you?' He wiped Angela's damp forehead. 'How do you feel?'

He looked, she thought, surprised, ill, grey-faced and sick.

'Wet,' she said, trying to take it lightly, and was caught on a betraying cough.

His mouth tightened. 'I'm not surprised. You'll be lucky if you escape pneumonia. Have you finished?' This last to Angela.

She nodded.

'I'm not going to ask you what happened. You and Boy run into the house and sit by the fire. I'll bring Lucy.'

He came across to her and looked down at her soaked and mud-stained figure with some grimness. 'There's blood on your face,' he said expressionlessly. 'And your arm.'

'I'm all right.' She struggled up unconvincingly and winced at a sudden pain in her shoulder.

'You're mad,' he said savagely. 'Why on earth didn't you come for me?'

'I sent Boy for you.'

'And plunged in yourself and got thoroughly beaten up for your pains. You little fool, don't you know the river's in flood?'

'I didn't think.'

'That figures.'

Her lip trembled. 'I'm sorry,' she whispered.

He bit off a violent exclamation and said with palpable self-restraint, 'Can you walk?'

Lucy took the hand he extended and got painfully to her feet. Apparently feeling this to be a sufficient answer, he swung her up in his arms without further ceremony and set off at a great pace towards the house.

'Oh, please,' she protested. 'There's no need. I'm just a little stiff.'

'Serve you right,' he snapped. 'I thought you were dead. When I looked round and you'd disappeared—' He broke off. 'One day,' he said, 'I will skin you alive.'

She laughed, coughed, and sneezed copiously. 'You're not very gallant,' she objected when she could get her breath.

'I don't feel gallant. I feel—'

'Furious?'

'More than that,' he assured her. 'Much, much more.'

They had reached the house and he kicked open the kitchen door and set her down by the Aga. It was blessedly warm and she clung to it. He looked at her a little helplessly.

'Now what? A bath, I suppose. And some dry clothes. You'll have to have my dressing-gown.'

'But Angela—' Lucy began, but was interrupted.

'Leave Angela to me. I'll bath her and find something to keep her warm for the time being. You go upstairs and start running your own bath. My dressing gown's on the bathroom door.'

'But Angela ought to go first . . .'

'I'll bath her down here in front of the stove. Unless,' with a grim, glittering look she mistrusted, 'you'd rather I come and bath you?'

She disclaimed hastily and did as she was bid. To be honest she was glad to do so. Her head throbbed and her whole body ached abominably. Inspecting herself in the bathroom mirror, she found a great disfiguring bruise beginning at her right temple which she was reasonably sure would end in a black eye of monstrous proportions. Considerably chastened, she went downstairs to find the others ensconced in the library before a blazing fire with a generous pot of cocoa standing in the hearth.

As Lucy went in they looked up and Robert began to pour some of the comforting liquid into a mug for her.

'Better?'

'Much,' she said gratefully.

She looked at him surreptitiously over the rim of her mug. Her first impression was confirmed. He was thinner, almost gaunt. And even now that that hard expression of anxiety was removed from his eyes he looked far from happy. In fact he looked worried to death.

Lucy tucked her bare feet under the skirts of his dressing gown. Robert noticed the movement.

'Cold?'

She glanced at the fire. 'Hardly. I shall be pretty well roasted by the time I've finished my cocoa. Do you always keep a fire fit to barbecue an ox?'

He laughed briefly. 'Usually. I find England singularly cold and depressing. The fire cheers me. I shall be glad to leave.'

She took a sip of cocoa. 'Oh, are you going abroad again?'

'Immediately after Christmas. I should be spending the New Year in Grenada.'

Her eyes widened. 'But what about Simone?' she exclaimed. 'Oh, I'm sorry, I didn't mean to pry. It's not my business. She just happened to mention . . . That is, I didn't think . . .'

He broke into her flurry of excuses, looking amused and alert suddenly. '*What* about Simone?'

'I—er—thought she was going away.'

He shrugged. 'I dare say she is. But not to Grenada. And not with me, I do assure you.'

'Oh.' Lucy tried unsuccessfully to look indifferent.

'Is that what you thought?' he demanded. 'That I was eloping with Simone Russell? But why, in heaven's name?'

She looked at her bare toes, blushing.

'Oh, I see. She told you so. What a very devious young woman she is, to be sure!'

Lucy swallowed. 'You were very good friends,' she said in a small voice.

'And so you believed her? What an innocent you are! She was anxious to make herself useful. She did. Useful,' he said emphatically, '*not* indispensable. She was a great help, one way and another.'

'And so you made use of her?' Lucy did not disguise her disapproval.

'She would have made use of me. It was a mutual arrangement. Don't you ever make use of people? Or no, I suppose you don't. It's usually the other way round, isn't it?'

'So you say.' She looked at Angela a-nod on the couch. 'They ought to be in bed, both of them. I'll get dressed and take them home.'

'You will not.'

At his masterful tone she bristled.

'Who will stop me?'

'I will.' He stood up. 'We have a discontinued conversation which I would like to reopen. Which I'm going to reopen. If you think those two brats need rest, I shall tuck them up in my own bed with my own electric blanket. But you don't go home until I say so.'

Lucy gaped at him.

'Understand?'

'Er—yes,' she agreed faintly. 'At least, I know *what* you're going to do, but I don't know why.'

'Because you think it's necessary,' he returned, scooping Angela out of her nest and collecting Boy from the hearthrug.

'But why can't we go home?'

He ground his teeth audibly. 'Because I want to talk to you,' he said slowly and distinctly.

'Oh.' She was nonplussed. Then she thought that, as he was quitting the country, he would want to settle Boy's future schooling before he went. 'About Boy, of course.'

He raised his eyes to heaven. 'Not about Boy. Not

about Angela. Not about the house or the garden or the village or anyone in it. About you. Wait here.'

She did.

Robert was back inside ten minutes. He found her huddled in her chair, her hands hidden in the sleeves of the dressing gown.

'Are you cold?' he asked with quick concern.

A smile lit her eyes briefly. 'Is that what you wanted to talk to me about? No, thank you. No more than I deserve to be.'

He sighed. 'Don't be a martyr. It's not your fault that Angela fell into the river.'

'How can you say that?'

'They were warned, both of them. I put the fear of God into them. You didn't approve, as I remember. And I believe you'd already told them to keep away from the river.'

'Yes.'

'So we'd both done as much as we could without actually driving a stake into the ground and tethering the little monsters to it. Some things they'll have to learn by experience. If they can't take them on trust. Like their aunt.'

'Me?'

He laughed, his eyes dancing at her outraged expression.

'You,' he mimicked. 'You don't take anything on trust, do you? You're as suspicious as a wildcat.'

'I don't see that you have any right to speak to me like that,' Lucy objected stiffly.

'And I don't see that you have any way of stopping me.' He took her face between his hands and smiled warmly down at her. 'You have to learn everything the hard way, don't you? Oh, Lucy, Lucy! You narrow-minded, bad-tempered, adorable fool. How long will it take you to find out that you don't want Browning? You want me.'

'No, I don't,' she snapped, adding with less conviction, 'I *can't*.'

'Not after God knows how many years of devotion to

the worthy Nicholas? Don't be so hidebound. Of course you can.'

'But I've only known you a matter of weeks,' she said distractedly. 'And most of that time you've been shouting at me or telling me off,'

'Then you shouldn't have been such a fool,' he replied. 'What else was I suppose to do, with you spilling your adolescent heart at Nicholas Browning's feet?'

'I've known him all my life,' she said slowly. 'He's part of my life. As for you—one can't fall in love in a matter of weeks.'

'In a matter of moments,' he averred. '*I* did, anyway.'

'*Did* you?' She was fascinated.

'Naturally. It was a new experience for me. I was rather proud of myself.' He laughed ruefully. 'Until I found that you counted yourself bespoke. You only talked to me when you couldn't avoid it or when your young man's bit of fluff was flirting with me. It was very lowering.'

'So you're going away?'

'Like all proper rejected suitors,' he nodded.

Lucy fell to inspecting her toes. 'I haven't noticed that you have been a suitor,' she pointed out.

'No. Well, I'll leave you to get over your adolescent passion for Nicholas until I come back. I'll do something about it then.'

'Or that you've been rejected,' she pursued, unheeding.

There was a little silence.

Then—'No,' he agreed thoughtfully. 'You have a point there.' He went down on one knee on the rug beside her. 'Dear Lucy. I have not been very considerate to you or very kind—which is unfair because you are a very kind and gentle girl yourself. My only excuse is that I was consumed with jealousy of all the people round you— the Brownings, the Lambs, the children. They were like walls I couldn't get past. You'd known them all your life and you loved them. There wasn't room for anyone new. I was distraught, so I was nasty. It's a bad habit I have when I don't get my own way.'

'Very childish,' she observed.

He took her hand and brushed his lips across it.

'Very,' he agreed. 'So—as you're so good with children—you might be able to deal with it better than most women, don't you think?'

She withdrew her hand, shaken. 'You don't think I am good with children,' she pointed out. 'You've been very voluble on the subject.'

'Simple envy,' he assured her. 'I've got a terrible temper.'

'And a nasty tongue.'

'I confess it.'

'And an intolerable habit of jumping to conclusions. And you talk so much you don't let anyone else get a word in edgewise.'

'I haven't noticed you trying to get a word in edgewise,' he retorted, stung. 'You usually clam up whenever I try to make conversation.'

'And you can't see what's going on under your nose. Nicholas asked me to marry him a week ago.'

'I see.'

'I,' said Lucy gently, 'refused.'

His reaction was unexpected. 'Why?'

'He'd been part of my life for too long. His place was fixed in my mind as the only man I would ever love—and suddenly I found he wasn't.'

Robert narrowed his eyes. 'You love a multiplicity?' he inquired politely.

'I wouldn't say that.'

'Then why?'

'I loved him—but not in the right way.'

'Which is?'

Lucy chuckled. 'Robert Challenger, you are a verbose and annoying man. The way I love you, I suppose.'

His reply was not verbal, but it was prolonged and satisfying. Some time later, when she was sitting beside him on the rug, her fingers twined in his and her head on his shoulder, he brushed her hair gently back from her face and murmured, 'Are you going to marry me after all?'

She turned her head to look into his eyes. He was smiling at her. She found she knew his face as well as her own, the firmness, the mischief, the wry self-mockery. And the intensity which was new and breathtaking. She gave a long happy sigh.

'When I'm asked,' she said.

romance is beautiful!

and Harlequin Reader Service
is your passport to the
Heart of Harlequin

Harlequin is the world's leading publisher of romantic
fiction novels. If you enjoy the mystery and adventure of
romance, then you will want to keep up to date on all of
our new monthly releases—eight brand new Romances
and four Harlequin Presents.

If you are interested in catching up on exciting and
valuable back issues, Harlequin Reader Service offers **a**
wide choice of best-selling novels reissued for your
reading enjoyment.

If you want a truly jumbo read and a money-saving value,
the Harlequin Omnibus offers three intriguing novels
under one cover by one of your favorite authors.

To find out more about Harlequin, the following
information will be your passport to the Heart of
Harlequin.

the omnibus

A Great Idea! Three great romances by the same author, in one deluxe paperback volume.

A Great Value! Almost 600 pages of pure entertainment for only $1.95 per volume.

Essie Summers

Bride in Flight (#933)
...begins on the eve of Kirsty's wedding with the strange phone call that changed her life. Blindly, instinctively Kirsty ran — but even New Zealand wasn't far enough to avoid the complications that followed!

Postscript to Yesterday (#1119)
...Nicola was dirty, exasperated and a little bit frightened. She was in no shape after her amateur mechanics on the car to meet any man, let alone Forbes Westerfield. He was the man who had told her not to come.

Meet on My Ground (#1326)
...is the story of two people in love, separated by pride. Alastair Campbell had money and position — Sarah Macdonald was a girl with pride. But pride was no comfort to her at all after she'd let Alastair go!

Jean S. MacLeod

The Wolf of Heimra (#990)
...Fenella knew that in spite of her love for the island, she had no claim on Heimra yet — until an heir was born. These MacKails were so sure of themselves; they expected everything to come their way.

Summer Island (#1314)
...Cathie's return to Loch Arden was traumatic. She knew she was clinging to the past, refusing to let it go. But change was something you thought of happening in other places — never in your own beloved glen.

Slave of the Wind (#1339)
...Lesley's pleasure on homecoming and meeting the handsome stranger quickly changed to dismay when she discovered that he was Maxwell Croy — the man whose family once owned her home. And Maxwell was determined to get it back again.

Susan Barrie

Marry a Stranger (#1034)
...if she lived to be a hundred, Stacey knew she'd never be more violently in love than she was at this moment. But Edouard had told her bluntly that he would never fall in love with her!

Rose in the Bud (#1168)
...One thing Cathleen learned in Venice: it was highly important to be cautious when a man was a stranger and inhabited a world unfamiliar to her. The more charm he possessed, the more wary she should be!

The Marriage Wheel (#1311)
...Admittedly the job was unusual — lady chauffeur to Humphrey Lestrode, and admittedly Humphrey was high-handed and arrogant. Nevertheless Frederica was enjoying her work at Farthing Hall. Then along came her mother and beautiful sister, Rosaleen, to upset everything.

Violet Winspear

Beloved Tyrant (#1032)
...Monterey was a beautiful place to recuperate. Lyn's job was interesting. Everything, in fact, would have been perfect, Lyn Gilmore thought, if it hadn't been for the hateful Rick Corderas. He made her feel alive again!

Court of the Veils (#1267)
...In the lush plantation on the edge of the Sahara, Roslyn Brant tried very hard to remember her fiancé and her past. But the bitter, disillusioned Duane Hunter refused to believe that she ever was engaged to his cousin, Armand.

Palace of the Peacocks (#1318)
...Suddenly the island, this exotic place that so recently had given her sanctuary, seemed an unlucky place rather than a magical one. She must get away from the cold palace and its ghost — and especially from Ryk van Helden.

Isobel Chace

The Saffron Sky (#1250)
...set in a tiny village skirting the exotic Bangkok, Siam, the small, nervous Myfanwy Jones realizes her most cherished dream, adventure and romance in a far-off land. Two handsome men determine to marry her, but both have the same mysterious reason....

A Handful of Silver (#1306)
...in exciting Rio de Janeiro, city of endless beaches and skyscraper hotels, a battle of wits is waged between Madelaine Delahaye, Pilar Fernandez, the jealous fiancée of her childhood friend, and her handsome, treacherous cousin — Luis da Maestro....

The Damask Rose (#1334)
...Vicki Tremaine flies to the heady atmosphere of Damascus to meet Adam Templeton, fiancé of the rebellious Miriam. But alas, as time passes, Vicki only becomes more attracted to this young Englishman with the steel-like personality....

information please

**All the Exciting News from
Under the Harlequin Sun**

It costs you nothing to receive our news bulletins and intriguing brochures. From our brand new releases to our money-saving 3-in-1 omnibus and valuable best-selling back titles, our information package is sure to be a hit. Don't miss out on any of the exciting details. Send for your Harlequin INFORMATION PLEASE package today.

MAIL COUPON TO ➤ Harlequin Reader Service,
M.P.O. Box 707,
Niagara Falls, New York 14302.

Canadian SEND Residents TO: ➤ Harlequin Reader Service,
Stratford, Ont. N5A 6W4

Please send me the free Harlequin Information Package

Name _____

Address _____

City _____

State/Prov. _____

Zip/Postal Code _____

ROM2005